ONE CRAZY WEEK

THE JETTY BEACH SERIES BOOK 2

CLAIRE KINGSLEY

Always Have LLC

This is a work of fiction. Any names, characters, places, or incidents are products of the author's imagination and used in a fictitious manner. Any resemblance to actual people, places, or events is purely coincidental or fictionalized.

Edited by Larks and Katydids

Cover by Kari March Designs

Published by Always Have, LLC

Previously published as Must Be Crazy: A Jetty Beach Romance

ISBN: 9781797050966

www.clairekingsleybooks.com

Created with Vellum

ABOUT THIS BOOK

One Crazy Week was originally published as Must Be Crazy: A Jetty Beach Romance.

It's not supposed to mean anything... until it does

The hot guy in a suit, sitting next to me at the bar? I don't know who he is, but when he tries to pick me up, he seems surprised when I sass him and turn him down. Truth? He's practically irresistible, and I almost say yes.

Turns out, he's Jackson Bennett, a cocky billionaire with a playboy reputation. And he has a very interesting proposition for me.

He wants to whisk me away for a week. No strings. No expectations. Just a crazy, lust-filled week of luxury with the hottest man I've ever met.

We come from different worlds, and it isn't supposed to mean anything. But the fire between us is scorching hot—in and out of the bedroom.

Our hearts are supposed to stay out of this, but apparently mine didn't get the memo. And when things get complicated —really complicated—it puts both of our hearts on the line.

1

MELISSA

I push the cart down the aisle, tossing in packages of markers, index cards, and ballpoint pens. School supplies—this is some sexy shit right here. The little drug store on the corner has an inexplicable early summer sale on school stuff, and I want to stock up my classroom.

When I was a student teacher, my supervisor told me I was getting into a profession that would require all of me: intellect, heart, and wallet. She wasn't wrong. But I budget for four or five big shopping trips a year, watch the sales, and manage to keep pencils and erasers in my students' grubby tween hands.

I pull my phone out of my pocket and check the screen, even though I know it hasn't dinged. It's a weird habit, borne of boredom more than anything. Now that the insane relief at finishing the school year has more or less blown over—I literally spent three days drunk off my ass after the last day of school—I find myself feeling antsy most of the time.

It's like being a kid again, growing up in a family with no siblings. Just me and my dad. Long summer days stretch out before me, full of boredom and possibility.

I wish I felt more of the possibility and less of the boredom.

My phone actually dings—a text from Nicole, my bestie. I smile. Despite the fact that she's newly engaged, I get to see a lot more of her since she moved back to Jetty Beach to live with her fiancé. It's great having her close by. We can do lunch, get together for drinks.

It's Friday, and I texted her earlier, hoping she'll be available to hang out later. I'm not interested in spending another Friday night on my couch with nothing but Netflix to keep me company.

Sorry Mel. Can't tonight. Dinner with the Jacobsens.

Damn. So much for that idea. *No worries. I'll catch up with you later.*

I finish shopping and my phone lights up again while I'm at the register. *I'm off work and free now. Coffee?*

I never say no to coffee. *Definitely. Meet you at Old Town.*

I drive my old Ford pickup to the little strip we call downtown, and find a parking space. I'm surprised. It's a Friday afternoon in the midst of the tourist season, and good spots are usually hard to come by.

People wander down the tree-lined sidewalks, some carrying shopping bags, others with ice cream cones. A cool breeze blows in off the water. I'm not close enough to see the beach, but there's no mistaking the place for anything but a beach town. Half the shops sell kites and windsocks, the other half beachy and nautical decor. Restaurants line the street—everything from my favorite coffee shop, the Old Town Café, to a great fish and chips place up the way.

Nicole just started working for the city a couple of weeks ago, and her office isn't far. I see her coming down the sidewalk, and wait outside the café for her to catch up.

Her blond hair hangs around her shoulders, held back

by sunglasses perched on her head. She's in a pretty cream blouse, a pair of light slacks, and cute baby blue heels that let her painted toenails show. Nicole always looks professional and put together. I glance down at my jeans and plain black t-shirt. I have flip-flops on my feet. But, meh, I'm not going to worry about it. It's not like I have anyone to impress.

"Hey." She flashes me her sunny smile. I love seeing her so happy. It makes up for her fiancé almost screwing things up.

We hug and go inside. After ordering our coffee, we pick a little table next to the window overlooking the street.

"So what's up with you?" I ask.

"You know, wedding stuff, work. The usual. How about you?"

"School supplies," I say, my tone wry.

"So exciting."

"It's really not." Nothing about my life is exciting lately.

"Met anyone recently?"

"Like, a guy? No, unfortunately. My social life includes you, Ryan, his brothers—who are nice enough guys, but not really my type—and ... yeah, that's it. I hang out with you guys."

Nicole laughs as the waitress sets down our coffee. "You need to get out more."

"Not everyone is going to fall down in front of the love of their life in a parking lot." That's how Nicole first ran into Ryan. "Although maybe I should just go out and get drunk tonight. It's not like I have anything else going on."

"Stop being so pitiful."

"I am not pitiful."

"Yes, you are. What about a dating app? You should make a profile. I can help if you want."

I groan. "Oh my god, do not even suggest that. I'm not going to try to meet a guy online. Are you serious?"

"Why not? It's not like you're going to meet someone down at Danny's Tavern."

"I might."

She arches an eyebrow. "Well, you can't exactly count on it."

"What's wrong with being single, anyway?"

"Nothing. You're the one who keeps complaining that your life is boring."

"Okay, fair enough. I'm just in a rut, I guess. I'm restless because I'm off work. Maybe I need a new hobby."

"That's a good idea."

"What the fuck kind of hobby would I have?" I say, laughing. "I don't think drinking Scotch qualifies."

Nicole laughs. Her phone makes a noise that sounds like wind chimes and she glances at the screen. "Hang on," she says while she types. "I'm just telling Ryan I'll be home in time to go to his parents' place for dinner."

I watch out the window, gazing at the people walking by. An elderly couple goes past, arm in arm. She's wearing a tacky fanny pack and they both have bright white sneakers. Across the street, a young couple stands next to a tree. The girl tilts her face up to the guy and he leans in to kiss her.

I sigh. I'm not much of a romantic, but I also haven't dated anyone in over a year. I miss being kissed.

I miss other stuff, too. A lot.

"Maybe I should ask Cody if he knows anyone who's single," Nicole says.

Cody is her fiancé's older brother. "I don't know, that's kind of weird."

"He's a doctor. Maybe he has some hot doctor friends."

"They're probably all married."

Nicole rolls her eyes. "Fine, since you don't want my help..."

"I'm sorry. Don't listen to me, I get restless every summer. Life is just always ... the same. I work my ass off all school year, which is fine. And then summer comes and goes. Work picks up again, and pretty soon another year is over. I'm going to wake up one day, realize I'm fifty, and I've never done anything."

"You need to get laid."

"Fuck yeah, I do." I love that I can talk to Nicole without holding back. "I need to get the shit fucked out of me hard core, but I don't see that happening anytime soon."

Nicole laughs, but I don't faze her. We've been friends since we were kids, so she's used to me. "Either that or I'm going to get you like, five cats, and you can resign yourself to being the crazy cat lady."

"I think the cats are more likely," I say. Nicole scowls at me. "Okay, okay, I'll stop moping. You know what, I'll even look at the online thing. I think it's probably a terrible idea, but I'll look at it."

"Yeah?" she says, her face brightening. "If it's dumb, you can just delete your profile."

"It has to at least be good for some laughs."

Later that evening, I settle down on my couch with some takeout Chinese and my laptop. I already regret telling Nicole I'll set up a profile on some dating site. But I know she'll call me tomorrow and ask if I did it. And what the fuck do I have to lose, anyway?

I pick one at random and fill in my information. I choose a profile picture that barely shows my face. I don't do social media at all—it feels too weird to have my personal information on the Internet. But I figure I can keep it vague enough to give it a try, and delete everything if I need to. It doesn't make me put in my last name, so I'll stay fairly anonymous.

I set up my profile, struggling to answer some of the questions. Interests? I'm a teacher, sure, but that's work. It isn't like I enjoy giving fifth grade math lessons in my spare time. I don't actually want to list drinking—that would send the wrong message, although I do enjoy a nice beverage. I throw in a few random things, like reading, beachcombing, and watching movies. I press enter, and it asks me to make sure my information is correct. It all looks kind of stupid, if you ask me, but I hit enter again.

I turn on a random reality show and eat my dinner on the couch. The sun starts to go down and the sound of seagulls carries through the windows. I glance at my laptop screen. The little notifications tab is highlighted on the dating site, so I click to see what it is.

Three replies to my new profile. That's interesting. I open the first one.

Hey, you're really gorgeous. Is that your real picture? Will you send me more pics? I need to know if that's really you. Are you fat?

I laugh so hard that I snort, and have to put my dinner down so I don't spill everywhere. Is this guy serious? I click on his profile. His username is godsgifttowomen69. This can't be real. It has to be a fake account, designed to punk people. His profile picture shows a heavyset man, probably in his thirties, with thick glasses and an awkward smile. He's so cliché, there's no way he's legit. I delete his message and open the next one.

Hi. I think we might have things of which are common. Fun times? Send me phone numbers. I text you.

Oh my god. I click on this guy. He has a shaved head and a tattoo on his face, just below his eye socket. His expression makes me wonder if he just murdered someone. He looks like a serial killer. I figure maybe he doesn't speak English very well, but his crazy eyes creep me the fuck out. I delete his message, too.

I open the third one and shriek, closing my laptop as fast as I can. The dude sent me a picture of his dick. His fucking dick. I shudder and push my laptop to the other side of the couch.

I am officially done with online dating.

I finish my dinner and clean up. I don't want to spend the night sitting around at home, so I grab my purse, slip on my flip-flops, and head out. I can walk to Danny's Tavern; it's only a few blocks away. It might not be a glamorous Friday night, but it beats sitting home alone—again.

And I need to get away from my laptop. I still don't want to open it. Some things you can't unsee.

2

JACKSON

I stand on the balcony of my penthouse hotel room, looking out over the water. This town doesn't have the sort of accommodations I'm used to, but my room isn't terrible. The view is amazing, even if the furnishings are rather pedestrian. I watch the sunset with a drink in my hand, the Pacific Ocean spread out in front of me. There's nothing wrong with that, although I regret not bringing someone along. The spacious room is too quiet, the room too empty.

I should have left town this afternoon. I intended to come down just for the day—I had a quick meeting with the art gallery owners, hammering out the details of the sale. For some reason, I decided to buy the Sunset Art Gallery in Jetty Beach. I spent a summer here as a kid and it's one of the only places that has good memories from my childhood. I like the idea of investing in the town, making it nice again. I didn't need to come in person, but I like this quirky little place. And fuck it, it's a Friday, and it isn't like anyone in the office can tell me no. A little ocean air sounded like a nice change.

But by about nine o'clock, I'm fucking bored. I figure my options are: drive home late, because I didn't have a driver take me out here, which sounds shitty; hang out in my hotel room drinking by myself, which sounds pathetic; or go out and see what people in this sleepy little town do on a Friday night.

Not much, it turns out.

I eat a mediocre dinner in the restaurant at my hotel. Alone, which isn't as terrible as I fear. Of course, the reasonably attractive waitress lingering at my table allows for some light conversation. But the novelty wears off pretty quickly and I find myself restless. I wander around the little downtown for a while, but everything is closed. I'm just about to give up when I see lights. A bar, and it's open. It looks ... dismal. A few cars out front, a neon sign in the window, the dark wood walls and door all blending together. It's not the sort of place I usually frequent.

But ... what the hell.

I push open the door. The inside isn't bad. It isn't good either, but it isn't the disgusting dive I expected. It's one of the few places in town that doesn't look like a beachside antique store threw up in it.

The light is dim, and a long bar takes up most of the back wall. On one side of the room, people play pool and toss darts. Most of the small tables on the other side of the room are taken. It's busier inside than I thought it would be, given the lack of cars out front; I guess a lot of people must walk.

I take a seat at the bar, glancing up at the liquor selection. Pretty standard. The bartender is nowhere in sight, so I pull out my phone and wait.

How I didn't notice the woman sitting down the bar, I have no idea. I look up and there she is. Dark hair pulled back in a messy bun, a tight black t-shirt showing the perfect curve of her breasts. Skinny jeans hug a shapely ass, and a pair of flip-flops dangles from her toes. She has a couple of empty shot glasses sitting in front of her. Her face turns toward me just enough to see the soft lines of her jaw, her full lips, dark eyes. A cute little nose. She's magnetic. Her tongue runs along her bottom lip and I can't help but smile. Finally, something in this town worth doing.

I'm just about to talk to her when the bartender appears in front of me. The guy fits the ambiance perfectly. Scruffy beard, shirt with the sleeves rolled up. If he was drying a glass with a white towel, it would be perfect.

"What can I get you?" he asks.

"Highland Park Thirty."

The bartender arches an eyebrow at me. "All right."

"Hold on there, Danny. He doesn't want the Highland Park Thirty."

I raise my eyebrows and look at the woman sitting at the bar. What the hell? "I don't?"

She purses her pretty lips and shakes her head. "Nope. Just because something's fucking expensive, doesn't always mean it's better."

"Then what *do* I want?" I ask, fascinated. I can't remember the last time anyone contradicted something I said. Except for Tammi. My assistant is sometimes too honest, but that's one of the reasons we have a good working relationship. Not everyone can handle me.

She scrutinizes me up and down. I love the way those brown eyes rove over me, like she's undressing me in her mind. Women do that to me all the time, but this one ... there's something different about the way she looks at me. And I won't lie; it's a fucking turn on.

"Glenlivet," she says. "But, Danny, don't even look at that

goddamn twelve-year-old. Give him the twenty-one." She moves her eyes back to me. "If you want to drop some cash, it ought to be worth it."

"All right. Make it two."

She smiles and shakes her head. "Thanks anyway. I'm fine over here by myself."

That sounds like a challenge.

"I insist. And I don't take no for an answer."

"One of those, huh?" she asks. "All right, captain. Danny, pour up."

"On the rocks," I add.

"Oh, no, no," she says with a maddening roll of her eyes. "Do not pour that lovely Scotch on ice."

Okay, now she's pissing me off. "Why is that?"

"Ice destroys the flavor." She sits up taller and scoots that hot little ass around on her stool. "The proper way to drink a good Scotch is straight up with a splash of water. A Scottish mineral water like Highland Spring is preferable, but since we're in Danny's Tavern, a bit of tap water will have to do."

I gape at her while Danny pours us each a measure of the Glenlivet twenty-one-year-old, adding a splash of water. I eye my glass while she takes her first drink. This woman wants to tell me how to drink Scotch?

Who the hell does she think she is? And why is this kind of turning me on?

I take a sip, fully expecting to put my glass down and argue with her. It slips down my throat, smooth as anything. Huh. It is good. I'm not sure how to feel about that.

She takes another drink and glances at me from the corner of her eye, a little smirk on her face.

Oh, hell no. She is not getting away with that.

I grab my glass and move down the bar to sit next to her. "Jackson Bennett," I say, holding out a hand.

She takes my hand and shakes it. Her grip is firm, but her hands are soft, almost delicate. What a contradiction she is, all curves and edges.

"Melissa Simon. Thanks for the drink, Jackson."

"The pleasure is all mine, Melissa." *The pleasure could be yours, if this goes well.*

"So what brings you to Jetty Beach?Since I know you aren't a local."

"Business."

"That's a very nonspecific answer. What sort of business?"

Wait, does she not know who I am? "Development, investments. I have my hands in a lot of different things. I'm working on a deal down here, and it could be the first of several."

"Sounds fascinating."

"And what is it you do, Melissa Simon?"

"I'm a teacher. Fifth grade."

This just keeps getting better. She's a schoolteacher? Hot for teacher, indeed. My dick stirs in my pants. "Do you teach in town?"

"Yep. Born and raised here. What about you? Where are you from?"

"I grew up in Chicago, but now Seattle. I live on Queen Anne."

She smiles, but doesn't look particularly impressed. She'd be impressed if she saw the view. I try a new angle. "So, how do you know so much about Scotch?"

A new smile crosses her face. There's depth behind that smile. "My daddy. His little girl was not going to grow up to drink Scotch on the rocks. He fucking raised me right."

"What does your daddy do for a living?"

"He's a commercial fisherman."

"I guess that's why you drink Scotch straight up and have a mouth like a sailor."

"Mouth like a fisherman. Sorry about that. My ability to censor myself is eaten up during the school year." She holds up her drink. "And drinking brings out the worst in me."

"No need to apologize. What kind of fish?"

"Excuse me?"

"What kind of fish does your daddy catch? When he's being a commercial fisherman."

People wonder why I'm successful, but it's pretty simple. A lot of it comes down to being able to read people. Melissa's eyes light up when she talks about her dad. It will work in my favor to ask personal questions she feels good about answering.

"Crab in the winter, longlining for black cod and halibut in the summer. He goes salmon fishing when they're in season, mostly just to fill our freezers though. And he smokes it. Oh my god, his smoked fish is to die for."

"Is it? I can't say I'm a fan." I'm lying. I loved smoked salmon. But I want to see what she'll say.

She arches her eyebrow at me. "Oh, captain, you have a lot to learn."

"Maybe you'll have to teach me."

She laughs a little, but I can tell I'm getting to her. I keep my eyes on her, not bothering to hide that I'm staring.

"What?"

"I was just wondering how I got so fortunate to find you here tonight. Alone."

Her eyebrows draw together. She looks … amused. "Bored on a Friday night, I guess."

"You don't have anyone to take you out?"

"If you're trying to find out whether I have a boyfriend, I don't. But don't get too excited."

I lean closer to her. Little strands of hair fall around her neck and she trails a finger on the rim of her glass. Long, dark eyelashes frame her eyes, and she wears almost no makeup that I can see. She is absolutely nothing like the women I usually date, with their manicures and foiled hair and fussy wardrobes. The women I spend time with are beautiful. But this woman, she smolders. She radiates sex appeal.

And I have the feeling she has no goddamned idea how hot she is.

"You're coming back to my hotel with me later." I'm absolutely confident. When I want something, I get it. And right now, I want Melissa Simon.

She shifts toward me and raises her eyebrows. "Is that so?"

"Definitely."

She tosses back the rest of her Scotch. "Usually men don't go straight for the kill like that. Don't you want to build up to it first?"

"Not particularly. I don't like to waste time."

She stands up from her stool and shoulders a small handbag. "Sorry to disappoint you, Jackson Bennett, but I'm not going back to your hotel with you."

She is *not* turning me down. I touch her on the arm, my hand gentle. She's already on the defensive. I need to coax. Her skin feels exquisite beneath my fingertips, making me want her all the more.

"I think you are."

She meets my eyes, utterly fearless. "Thanks for the drink, captain." She turns and walks away, leaving me gaping at her.

3

MELISSA

I walk out the door, my heart beating so fast I can barely breathe. What just happened in there? One minute I was sitting at the bar, pathetically alone, trying to ignore the dipshit hitting on the girl at the table behind me. The next minute, I'm telling some guy what kind of Scotch to drink.

And he was literally the hottest man I have ever seen in my entire life. The kind of man you don't see in places like Jetty Beach, or anywhere that actually exists. If I looked at him straight on before I spoke up, I doubt I would have been able to get a word out. He would have ordered his stupid expensive Scotch and been on his way, leaving me a drooling idiot in his wake.

But I *did* talk to him, like a crazy person. I told him what to drink, and how to drink it. Of course, I'm fucking right. But that's beside the point. He looked at me like I grew a second head.

And then moved to sit next to me.

I keep walking, fast, away from Danny's Tavern. I don't think I can handle it if he follows me out. The walk to my house isn't long, and it's a good thing I didn't drive. The few drinks aside, my head is spinning. I'm not sure how it's possible, but he smelled better than he looked. His clothes fit perfectly, straining just slightly in all the right places. *All* of them. Broad shoulders, strong arms, and I knew he had a set of delicious abs under that button down shirt.

I've never met a man who was so instantly appealing.

It was fun trading a little flirty banter with him. Until he told me, flat out, that I was going back to his hotel with him. That made me stop in my tracks. I wasn't offended. I liked his bold attitude. He was cocky as shit, and that shouldn't have turned me on. But it did.

I left because I was fucking scared.

When he uttered those words, I wanted nothing more than to do exactly what he said. This feeling swelled up inside me, a burning need. In half a second, I imagined it all: following him to his car, letting him drive me to his hotel, going with him into his room, enjoying a night of mind-blowing sex with this perfect specimen of a man.

I'll probably never have a chance like that again. I'm not usually one to jump in the sack with a guy the first time we meet (those few one-night stands in college aside). I love good sex as much as anyone, and holy shit it has been too long, but running off to sleep with a stranger is a stretch for me.

Except with Jackson Bennett, I wanted to. Oh my god, I wanted to.

And when he touched my arm... I don't even know what that was, but it made me feel like I was melting.

I hug myself against the chill night air. He was overwhelming, filling my senses. And son of a bitch, my panties are so wet I'll need to change when I get home. Tonight might be a night for my little battery-powered buddy. I'm so agitated, I don't think I'll be able to sleep.

A few cars pass, and my back clenches each time. Is it him? If I see him again, if he looks at me with those insane blue eyes, I know I'll be powerless to refuse him. And that thought terrifies me.

By the time I make it home, I'm pretty convinced I imagined the whole thing. There's no way that man was in Danny's Tavern. And if he was, there's no way he talked to me. And furthermore, if he did talk to me, it's impossible that he wanted me to come to his hotel with him.

No way. It didn't happen.

I shuffle inside and toss my phone on the couch, heading straight for bed. A shower sounds good, but there's the slightest whiff of his cologne lingering on me. It's probably in my hair. It didn't happen—Jackson Bennett did not exist—but I'm not quite ready to let go of the dream.

I GET up the next morning feeling more like myself. After a little DIY time last night, I went to sleep fairly relaxed. I try not to think about the fact that I dreamed of a mysterious man with piercing blue eyes all night. It's over, and I didn't take the chance. On to the rest of my life.

My phone rings, and I pick it up, sitting down on the couch and putting my feet up. I really need to change my ringtone. This one is getting old. It's Nicole.

"Hey, Nic. What's up?"

"Hey, did you get my email?"

"Um." I open my laptop, squinting so I don't have to see the dick pic again, and close out of the dating site. I click on my email. "Just saw it."

"Okay, no big deal. I just sent you some ideas for bridesmaid dresses."

Right. Bridesmaid dresses. Lovely. I love that she asked me to be her maid of honor, but fancy dresses aren't really my thing. And isn't the wedding, like, next year? "Cool, I'll take a look. But you know this isn't my area, right? Just tell me what to wear and I'll cope with it."

Nicole laughs. "Sure, but I want you to love it, too. Or, if you refuse to love it, I want you to be comfortable. Anyway, I think all the ones I sent would look amazing on you."

"Whatever you say."

"So, what did you do last night?"

"I made a profile on a dating app."

"Awesome. Did you get any messages?"

"Um, yes. Three. A socially awkward guy who wants to know if I'm fat, and a serial killer."

"Oh shut up, he wasn't a real serial killer."

"He looked like one. He had a face tattoo, Nic."

"Ew. You said there were three. Who was the third?"

I start laughing before I can even tell her. "He sent me a dick pic."

"A what?"

"He sent me a picture of his junk."

"No."

"I swear."

"Wow. That's horrifying. Now I feel bad for suggesting you do that."

"It really was horrifying, but it's okay. It's not your fault some guys shouldn't be allowed to have contact with other humans. I ended up going out for a couple drinks at Danny's." I pause. Should I tell her? Why the fuck not. "A hot guy bought me a drink."

"Ooh," Nicole says, her voice going all squee-ish. "Tell me more."

"Eh, there's not much to tell. This guy came in and tried to order a stupid expensive scotch. So like a dumbass, I jumped in and told him not to order it."

"That sounds like you."

"Yeah, he looked at me like I was nuts, but whatever. I told him what to order and he insisted on buying one for me."

"And...?"

"And, nothing. We talked for a little while and I left."

"Didn't you even get his number? Or give him yours?"

"No." But shit if I don't regret it.

"Well that sucks."

"It kinda does. 'm not gonna lie, he was fucking gorgeous."

"Then why did you leave?"

"He looked right at me and said, 'You're coming with me to my hotel later.' And damn it, Nicole, I had to prove him wrong." More to the point, I had to get myself out of there before I did exactly what he wanted.

"Wow, bold."

"I know." And way more of a turn-on than I want to admit. "Oh well. He was amusing and the Scotch was good."

"Did Mr. Expensive Scotch have a name?"

"Yeah," I say, trying to remember. "Jack. No, Jackson. Was it Benson? No, Jackson Benson sounds weird."

"Jackson Bennett?"

"Hey, good guess. That was it. Jackson Bennett. Wait, how did you know that?"

She goes silent.

"Nicole?"

"Did you just tell me that Jackson Bennett bought you a drink at Danny's last night?" she asks.

"Yes..."

"You're sure it was him?"

"Sure it was who?"

"Jackson Bennett."

"That's what he said. Why, am I supposed to know him from somewhere?"

"You've never heard of Jackson Bennett?"

"Um, no. Why would I?"

"Only you, Melissa. I don't even know how to explain him to you. Just Google him."

I groan, but type in his name. Half a second later, the page loads. "Holy shit."

"Right?"

I scroll through the results and my throat tries to close up. There he is, smirking at me from a hundred angles. This is definitely him. "Is that a magazine cover?"

"Yep."

"Listen to this. *Jackson Bennett is one of Seattle's most eligible bachelors, but will a woman ever be able to tame his wild ways? Known for his lavish parties and late night excursions, as well as his tell-all Twitter feed, Jackson Bennett is one to watch.* What is this guy, some kind of rich playboy?"

"That's exactly what he is. I can't believe you've never heard of him."

"You're surprised? This isn't the sort of thing I pay attention to."

"Go to his Twitter feed."

"I don't do Twitter."

"That's not the point," she says. "Just look."

I bring up Twitter and fumble around, trying to figure out how to search.

"Did you find him?"

"Hang on." I find his name, and that is definitely his profile picture. Clicking on it brings a line of tweets, or whatever they're called. Some are just text, others are photos. In one, he's surrounded by bikini clad women, in another he's holding a glass of champagne, that little smirk on his face.

"Holy shit, Mel, look at his tweets from last night."

I scroll back up.

Flying solo at the beach. Boring as fuck. Heading out to find ... something. #lonewolfontheprowl

"Lone wolf on the prowl? Who is this guy?"

Nicole laughs. "He has a huge following. Look at all those comments."

I roll my eyes. The comments are a mix of women throwing themselves at him, and men giving him the equivalent of a bro fist.

"Oh, what the fuck."

Jetty Beach not without the hotness. Sassy girl schooled me on Scotch. The tweet is followed by a lot of requests for pictures.

"Oh my god, is that you?" Nicole asks, practically squealing again. "You're *sassy girl*!"

"He twittered about me?" I try to sound mad, but it's kind of exciting.

"Oh, calm down. He didn't use your name or anything. He didn't even take your picture."

Who is this guy? Playboy isn't even the word. Half his twitter feed is filled with photos of him posing with gorgeous women at parties—the sort where people dress up and little lights twinkle in the background and they serve expensive drinks. What the fuck was he doing at Danny's bar? And more importantly, why did he talk to me?

"You should respond."

I laugh so hard I snort. "I don't Twitter, Nicole."

"The verb is *tweet*."

"Whatever."

"Create an account. Can you imagine how funny that would be? He'd never expect you to reply. Oh my god, make your user name sassy girl!"

"Seriously?" Although it does sound kind of fun. If he even notices my comment. There are so many people commenting on his tweets, mine will probably get lost in the shuffle. Still, there's no harm done if he never sees it. And if he does....

"Okay, fuck it, I'm doing it."

Nicole laughs again. "This is so great."

I fill out the information to create a profile. User name, @sassygirl555. "Do I have to have a profile picture?"

"Yeah, are you on your laptop?"

"Yes."

"Just find a picture you already have," Nicole says. "You can crop it or whatever."

"Ugh. Fine."

I don't want to put too much effort into this little stunt, so I find a picture that includes me, and crop it to my head and shoulders. Okay, so I do make sure it's a cute picture. But I don't scroll through my files looking for one that makes me look particularly sassy. Nope, not at all.

"Okay, apparently I am now on Twitter."

"Stop the world, I need to get off. I never thought I'd see the day."

"Clever. Okay, now what do I do?"

"Just click the little button that lets you reply to his tweet."

"But what should I say?"

"Obviously something sassy," she says.

"Oh, obviously. But I'm not using a stupid hashtag."

I stare at the screen for a second, then type in a reply and hit enter. *Hey, what's a sassy girl to do? You needed some schooling, captain.*

"Captain?" she asks.

"Yeah, I don't know. That's what I called him last night."

"So flirty."

"Now what?"

"Now we wait to see if he replies."

A man's voice says something in the background and Nicole answers. It sounds like she's holding the phone away from her. She giggles and goes silent.

"Gross, Nicole," I say, raising my voice. "Stop making out while you're talking to me."

I *am* happy for her, but those two. They can't keep their hands off each other and don't seem to care who's around. Or on the phone.

I am definitely not jealous. Not at all.

"Sorry," she says with a laugh. "Okay, I have to go. Stop it, Ryan. Mel, put the Twitter app on your phone so you don't miss his tweets. Ryan, you're so bad. I'm on the phone. Mel, text me when he replies."

"Okay." I try not to sound too enthusiastic, but a thrill runs through me, imagining the look on Jackson's face when he sees I tweeted back at him. Will it make him smile that crazy hot smirk?

It's silly, and I know it. Jackson Bennett lives in a world I'm not sure is real. Whatever happened last night, and any subsequent tweeting that occurs, will be nothing more than a funny story in a day or so.

4

JACKSON

I'm up early. Last night's lack of activity had me in bed at an absurd hour, especially for a Friday night. The upside is, I check out of the hotel and get on the road before nine. And the lack of hangover is refreshing. I figure I'll be home by noon, with plenty of time to go over some paperwork my assistant left on my desk. And I need something to do tonight. Fuck if I'm going to sit around by myself two nights in a row.

Last night was such a disappointment that I didn't even check Twitter. I have a shit-ton of followers and I tweet constantly. My brother sends me angry emails, ranting at me about my 'antics.' He says I'm sullying the family name. I don't bother telling him that's half the fun of it.

The whole Twitter thing is nothing—it's just a diversion to amuse myself. Okay, so I *do* like the attention. Wherever I go, I have women throwing themselves at me to make it into my Twitter feed. There isn't anything wrong with that. I live an amazing life and I have nothing to hide. Why not have some fun with it and bring people along for the ride?

Of course, I only tweet the good stuff. People don't care

about the board meetings and negotiations, the contracts and late nights in the office. They like to see the parties, the women, the hot cars, the exotic destinations. And, to be fair, those are the fun parts of my life.

I pick up my phone and scroll through my feed with my thumb, keeping one eye on the road. I tweeted about Melissa before I left the bar last night. I hedged the truth—I'm not going to admit publicly to being turned down. I wish I took a picture of her. As soon as she left the bar, I searched for her online. Nothing. She isn't on social media, and if she is, she has her shit so locked down the fucking NSA won't be able to find her. I Googled her name and found a mention of her in a local newspaper article—something about raising money for school supplies—but that's all.

I still can't believe she walked away from me last night. When was the last time I struck out with a woman? Sure, I get turned down sometimes. That's the risk you take for boldness. But the number one reason—no, the *only* reason—I ever get a "no" is that the woman is already in a relationship. Melissa told me she doesn't have a husband or a boyfriend, so that isn't the problem. She simply said *no*.

It pisses me off, but it makes her all the more intriguing.

I scroll through the comments on last night's tweets and almost drive off the road.

Hey, what's a sassy girl to do? You needed some schooling, captain.

Son of a bitch. It's definitely Melissa. I recognize that irresistible mouth, those smoldering dark eyes, that saucy smile. And she called me *captain* again. She must have looked me up and found my Twitter feed.

I race up the freeway, a plan already coming together in my mind. I don't have her address, but how hard can that be to find? I call Tammi and give her Melissa's name, with instructions to find a mailing address for her. Tammi's amazing at that sort of thing. By the time I get home to my condo, I'll have an email with Melissa's whole life laid out in front of me.

Oh, Melissa. The things I am going to do to you.

5

MELISSA

I know I'm in trouble when the twenty-one-year-old bottle of Glenlivet shows up at my house. No note, no return address, no indication as to where it came from. Just a bottle of Scotch.

The Scotch I told Jackson to order at Danny's.

I pull it out of the box and set it on my counter, staring at it as if it might suddenly morph into something else—like a six-pack of Corona—and I can convince myself I imagined the Glenlivet. But it doesn't change. It just sits there, staring at me, mocking me with its mystery.

How did he find out where I live? I told him my name, and he can find me on Twitter. But other than the hastily made Twitter account, I have no online presence. I probably should be creeped out, but I can't stop smiling. It's so ... him. I don't even know him, but from our brief interaction, I know this is *so* Jackson. If he wanted to catch me off guard, he certainly succeeded. What does he expect me to do next?

What won't he expect?

An idea pops into my head. I'm probably going to regret it later, but I can't help myself. I open the bottle and pour myself a glass, adding a splash of mineral water. It is such a nice Scotch. I grab my phone, hold up the drink, and take a selfie.

I definitely do not take seventeen, trying to get the best angle.

Hoping I don't mess something up, I add the picture to Twitter and compose a tweet.

Straight up with a splash of mineral water—the real way to drink Scotch. Too bad I'm drinking alone.

I add his user name with that little @ symbol. I hope that's right. Then I click *Tweet*.

I put my phone down, already regretting the tweet. How many people are going to see it? This is so weird. Jackson never replied to my earlier message, and until the Scotch showed up, I assumed that whatever passed between us—if it was anything at all—was long over. But then he went to the trouble to send me the Scotch. As much as I want to be a little bit hipster in my attitude toward social media, this is starting to get fun.

I check my phone a few times to see if he replied, but there isn't anything from him. Someone retweeted my tweet —why the fuck did they do that?—and a few others seemed to have "liked" it. Although I guess that's a good thing in Twitter-land, it reminds me that this stupid little flirtation is enormously public. Not like I give a shit what these weirdos think. I'm only messing with him, anyway.

I refresh the app one more time and a little spike of nerves runs through my tummy. He replied.

Gorgeous. And the Scotch looks good too.

Really? That's the best he can do?

Wait, what does that mean? I thought he'd acknowledge sending it, say "You're welcome," somehow. Was it him?

He must have sent it. I don't know anyone else who would anonymously ship me good Scotch.

The little envelope icon lights up with a "1". What is this? I tap it and a new window opens. It's a private message.

Don't drink the whole bottle, sassy girl. I expect you to share.

I grin. Oh you do, do you? *That's a tall order, captain. It's a good Scotch.*

A new message. *I guess I better come soon.*

My heart beats faster at the thought of seeing him again. He isn't serious. Is he? He isn't going to come down here to see me. Do I want him to? *I guess you better.*

Oh shit, what did I just do? That's a pretty fucking obvious invitation. A little back and forth online is one thing. But what if I see him again and can't maintain control? What if I melt into a big puddle of stupid in the presence of that delicious body?

I try to tell myself I'm tougher than that, but I'm honestly not sure.

THREE DAYS LATER, I haven't received any messages, and no more mysterious packages turned up on my porch. I'm annoyed with myself for spending so much time checking Twitter. Not only do I look to see if he messages me again, I watch for his tweets. There isn't much. No parties, no groups of beautiful women. Since he sent me the Scotch, he mostly tweets about food.

I have to admit to an odd fascination with his food porn. Are those really pictures of what he's eating, or is he taking them from food magazines? More than anything else, it makes me hungry. This guy eats like a fucking king.

I sit on my couch with a big mug of chamomile tea, half

watching a movie and half flipping through the pages of a magazine. I just had lunch with Nicole, which should have been a nice diversion. Instead, we obsessed over Jackson the entire time. She saw my tweet with the glass of Scotch—because of course she did—and wanted to know what else is happening. I think she was disappointed to hear we only messaged back and forth a couple of times and I haven't heard from him since.

I try to convince her I'm not disappointed, but I know she isn't buying it. Neither am I.

There's a knock at my door and my stomach does a somersault. I'm not expecting anyone. My dad is in town, but he never stops by unannounced. And I just saw Nicole.

I answer the door to find a large unmarked box and a Fed Ex guy jogging back to his truck. The box is pretty heavy, but I manage to get it inside. There isn't anything on the outside other than my name and address. No indication what it is or where it came from.

Okay, here goes. I grab a pair of scissors and cut through the thick tape. Inside, I find reams of white paper, a huge case of number two pencils, a big package of washable markers, a case of crayons, and a shit-ton of Elmer's glue.

My heart sinks right into my stomach. It's just a school supply donation. They come in every so often, usually when a local business needs a last-minute tax deduction. Although they're typically sent to the school, not to my house.

I dig through the box, looking for a note or a letter, anything to tell me who sent it. At the bottom, I find a folded piece of paper. It's a printed-out newspaper article from about a year ago. Our local paper did a feature on the school district's budget issues. They interviewed me, and I gave them a few quotes about how teachers use their own money to make sure their classrooms have adequate supplies all year. At the top is a photo of me with a few of my students, holding up some of the donated school supplies we received.

No fucking way.

Is this from Jackson? It can't be. I did tell him I'm a teacher, and anyone could Google my name and find that article. Would he have done this?

I think about tweeting another picture, but what if he didn't send the package? It seems next to impossible that it was him, and I'll feel pretty stupid when he tweets back with a big "WTF is that?"

I put the stuff back in the box and grab my phone, wondering if I should ask him. There's a little notification on the Twitter icon, so I check, expecting to see another pointless retweet of my Scotch picture.

It's a message from Jackson.

What do you think? Did you open it? Did I choose the right stuff? I don't really know anything about kids.

I stare at my phone, my mouth wide open. There is no way Jackson Bennett, billionaire playboy, sent me a box of fucking school supplies.

It seems insane that he messaged me so soon after it was delivered. *How did you know I got it?*

I set up surveillance on your house.

What? I run to the window and look out, fully expecting to see a utility van or some shit parked outside. But the street is empty.

I check my messages again. *I got a delivery notification from Fed Ex.*

Leaning my head back, I put a hand on my forehead. I am such a dork. Surveillance. I'm not going to admit he fooled me with that one.

I send him another message. *This is actually pretty amazing. Did you really send all of it?*

I'm glad you like it. You haven't given me much to work with.

What is that supposed to mean?

It feels like ages before he replies. *There are only four things I know about you. You like good Scotch. You teach 5th grade. Your daddy is a fisherman. And I can't stop thinking about you.*

My chest tightens and I cover my mouth. He cannot be serious. *Are you fucking with me?*

I was wrong. Five things. You have a mouth like a sailor. Less than a second later, another message. *I won't fuck with you. I might do other things, but fuck *with* you isn't one of them.*

I sink down on the couch, bewildered. My heart races, and I'm all hot between the legs. School supplies. This man managed to make school supplies the sexiest fucking thing in the universe.

Now I know I want to see him. I *need* to see him. I need to reach out and touch him to make sure he's real. Because at this point, it all feels like a crazy dream.

6

MELISSA

Jackson and I talk back and forth for days. At first it's all Twitter. He mentions me in some of his tweets, usually when they're pictures of his drinks.

A glass of Scotch—without ice. *What do you think, @sassygirl555? Could the Longmorn top the Glenlivet 21?*

A frosty mug of beer, sitting on an outdoor table. *Some nights are beer nights. I think* @sassygirl555 *would agree.*

A thin slice of the most decadent-looking chocolate torte I've ever seen. *Dessert for one. @sassygirl555*

That last one makes my breath catch. Am I reading too much into it, or does it mean he wishes he was having that dessert with me?

He sends me a lot of private messages, too, until he declares his Twitter app "annoying" and asks for my number so he can text me. I balk for a moment at giving it to him, then roll my eyes at myself. He figured out where I live. Why should I worry about whether he has my phone number?

We text each other every day. He asks about my day or

what I'm doing. Sometimes he texts about work—complaining about idiots he has to deal with, or saying he had a meeting that went well. He asks random questions, like whether I like chocolate (yes), or sushi (no), or am a vegetarian (hell, no).

Our brief conversations usually go from small talk to playful banter. He teases me about living in the sticks. I hit back with quips about him being a suit. We talk about movies and music. I find myself looking forward to those little moments, the short messages shining at me from my phone screen. One morning I panic, realizing I forgot to charge my phone overnight and the battery is dead. I'm as excited as a fucking kid at Christmas when I manage to get the phone to turn on again and find he texted me twice.

The following Thursday—thirteen days after I met Jackson at Danny's, and no I'm not counting—I wake up to my phone dinging with a text. I smile before I even look. Of course it's him.

Got up for an early meeting that took five minutes. Assholes.

I laugh. *That's shitty. You should charge them more money somehow.*

Good plan. I think I will.

God, why do his texts make me feel all tingly? He's telling me about a meeting, for fucks sake. That shouldn't turn me on. *Well, now you're up and you can tweet pictures of your decadent breakfast.*

I'd rather be doing something else.

I lay back against my pillow. I want to see where this goes. *Tell me.*

Do you really want to know?

Yes. Tell me.

There's a pause before his next message. *If I had my way,*

I'd start at your toes. I'd inch my way up your body with my lips. My tongue. My teeth. Do you want to hear more?

Fuck yes, I want to hear more.

I'd get to your thighs and I'd gently push open your legs. I'd use my tongue—I'm very good with my tongue. I wouldn't stop until you screamed my name.

Oh my god. Is he for real? *Don't stop there. We're just getting started.*

I'd flip you over and push my cock inside you. You'd be so hot and wet. I'd grab your hips and pound my cock into you—harder and deeper than you've ever had before.

My breathing quickens. This is getting intense, fast. *Don't stop, Jackson. I want more.*

Fuck yeah, you want more. I'd bring us both to the brink of climax and then I'd make you wait. I'd pull out and stop. Push in again. Out. In. I'd turn you over so I could put my mouth on your breasts while I fuck you. I'd run my tongue over your nipples and grab your ass while you shudder with pleasure beneath me.

I am shuddering, all right. He has me going crazy and all he's doing is texting me. Is this sexting? The idea sounded so dumb, but this is hot as fuck.

That's right, captain. You give me that hot, throbbing cock and show me how it's done.

Melissa, I'm about to get in my car and drive down there right now.

Oh shit, is he serious? *You are?*

Fucking hell, I can't. Meetings that I can't blow off.

Damn it. Heat builds between my legs, and my panties are wet. Even if he was able to leave, he's three hours away. And can I honestly say I'd do it? After a couple weeks of tweets and texts, would I really let this man fuck me?

Yes. Yes, I would.

I take a deep breath and rub my hands over my face to calm down. This is one way to wake up.

I text him back, feeling like I need to cool this off. *That sucks. Would have been good. Too bad you live so far away.*

Too bad is right. Shitty. Pretty sure I'm going to have to lock my office door and jack off before I can concentrate on work. I can't think of anything but you.

That makes me laugh. I don't know why I find it so funny. Maybe because it seems so ridiculous. I've seen his Twitter feed—the constant parade of women. He's as charming as the fucking devil, and I have no idea if he's any more trustworthy.

Still, I can't think of anything but him either.

SATURDAY MORNING, I stop by my dad's house. He's about to leave for a fishing trip. He'll be gone for a week, maybe ten days, and I like to check in with him before he leaves, when I can. He assures me his back is holding up fine—he tends to have pain these days—and I can tell he isn't lying. So I wish him well, give him his customary kiss on the cheek for good luck, and head home.

I turn onto my street and see a car parked out in front of my house. To be fair, "car" hardly seems like the right word. I have no idea what it is—I don't recognize the logo. Bugatti? I've never heard of it, but it's the hottest car I've ever seen. And I know instantly who it is.

My belly tumbles with a sudden case of madly flying butterflies. I almost drive my truck right by without stopping. How long has he been here? I glance at my phone. He hasn't texted. At the last second, I turn up the driveway and pull into my garage. I let the garage door close behind me and go inside. I need a second to catch my breath.

The knock comes as I set my purse down on a side table. I swallow hard and my heart beats so furiously I'm sure it will echo. The curtains on the front window are closed, so I can't see him. I walk to the door, my hands trembling. Why am I so nervous?

Should I count the reasons?

I open the door and there he is. He looks incredible, dressed in a cream button-down shirt with the top two buttons decadently undone, and a pair of sleek gray slacks. Piercing blue eyes, his jaw covered in stubble, his lips parting over his perfect teeth in a smile. He looks like he stepped out of a fucking magazine. Which he kind of has; I saw his Seattle Weekly cover.

"Hi, Melissa," he says.

I glance down at my own clothes. Jeans—at least they aren't ripped—and a slim black tank top. My feet are bare; I kicked off my sandals when I came inside.

"Hi," I say. His eyes bore into me, like he's going to make no effort to look away. I meet his gaze and my tummy does another flip-flop. "This is a surprise."

"Do you like surprises? I guess I should have asked that."

I do, actually. I'm stunned, but also thrilled. "Yeah, surprises are good. Sorry, I'm just still trying to process the fact that you're standing on my doorstep."

"I know, I am too."

Let him in, dumbass! "Oh, god, sorry. Do you want to come in?"

"Thank you."

He slips through the door, coming so close I can smell him. His scent almost makes my eyes roll back. It's subtle, but so rich and masculine. I barely resist the urge to run my hand across his chest as he walks by me.

He puts his hands in his pockets and glances around. "Cute place."

"Thanks." Shit, what am I supposed to do now? Offer him a drink? It's ten o'clock in the morning. Ask him to sit down? See if he wants me to rip his clothes off? "Um, do you want some coffee?"

"Coffee would be great."

I go into the kitchen and stand there for a moment, not seeing anything. Is Jackson Bennett actually in my house? This is too strange for words. I blink hard to rouse myself from my stupor and put on some coffee. Suddenly, I wish I had a Keurig or something that would make coffee faster. I fidget, twirling my fingers while I wait for it to brew.

I pour two mugs, fill a little pitcher with cream, and add my grandma's old sugar bowl, all on a wood tray. I bring it out to the living room to find Jackson leaning back on my couch, one ankle crossed over his knee, his arms stretched across the back cushions.

"Wow," he says. "I didn't expect you to go to all this trouble."

"It's no trouble." I put the tray on the coffee table.

He takes one of the mugs and pours in some cream, then offers to pour mine. I hold out my mug for him, then add a little sugar. The act of doing something so mundane as making coffee with a man who looks like a fucking model is insane.

I sit down, my legs angled toward him. He takes a sip of his coffee, his posture so relaxed it's like he does this every Saturday morning. His nonchalance puts me at ease, and I tuck my legs up and settle back into the cushions, cupping my mug in my hands.

"So, how was the drive?" I ask.

"Long. I woke up early this morning and decided, you know what, fuck it, I'm going."

"You decided to come down here just this morning?"

He looks at me with that ridiculous smirk. "Yep."

"Wow. Well, I guess it's a little early for Scotch."

"That's all right. I don't have anything on my schedule."

Just as I'm about to ask if he considered whether I might have anything on *my* schedule, he speaks up again.

"What about you? Am I interrupting a busy day?"

"No, not really."

"Good," he says, his grin widening. "I've really been looking forward to seeing you again. Our last meeting was too short."

"Well someone came on a little strong."

"I know. I can't remember the last time someone told me what I should order at a bar."

I give him a playful smack on the shoulder. "Okay, captain."

He puts his coffee down and adjusts so he's facing me. "I love it when you call me that."

Oh, fuck yes. Here we go. My belly flips again and my fingers tingle. I want to touch him, but I'm afraid to move.

"It seems like it suits you. I take it you're used to being the boss."

"I am."

His eyes rove up and down. How can he just stare at me like that? He's so intense, but his eyes positively dance. Is he imagining what he wants to do to me? I hope he'll start acting on it soon. My blood is pumping, and my panties are getting wetter by the second.

"You know what, I have an idea."

"What's that?"

"What are you doing this week?"

I blink at him in confusion. "This week? Like, what am I doing every day?"

"Yeah. Do you have plans this week? Anything you can't get out of?"

"No, not really. I'm off work for the summer."

"That's perfect." His mischievous smile grows and he pulls out his phone, taps a few buttons, and holds it up to his ear. "Hey, Tammi. Yeah, good. Listen, clear my schedule for the week. Yes, the entire week. I'm taking off and I won't be reachable. No, they'll have to reschedule. That one, hmm ... no, I can cancel that. It won't matter in the long run. Yes, I know that will be a tight deadline, but you have everything you need from me already, don't you? I thought so. Okay, so we're good, then. Perfect."

He hangs up and smiles at me again. He looks like a kid who just found out his parents are leaving him alone for the weekend.

"What was that about?"

"Come away with me," he says. "Just for a week. We can go anywhere. The sky's the limit. Let me take you on an adventure. It will be amazing, I promise."

I gape at him. Just when I think he can't be any more surprising. "Are you serious? Why would I do that?"

He leans closer. "Let's be honest with each other. No bullshit. I think you're fucking incredible and I can't stop thinking about you. And I know you can't stop thinking about me. Let's just be crazy. Let's take off and leave the real world behind for a while. It's just a week. I've been dying, wanting to see you again. Give me a week, then I'll bring you home."

"Honest? No bullshit?"

He nods.

"You're right. I haven't been able to get you out of my head. But this is ... this is crazy."

"Yep." He keeps smiling at me, his eyes crinkling at the corners.

"Just a week?"

"Yes."

"Then you'll bring me home?"

"Exactly."

"No strings?"

"Not a one. We'll go, have fun, come back. Life goes on."

This isn't just crazy. It's absolute insanity. I can't just run off with Jackson at a moment's notice.

Or can I?

I'm single, and I don't have to go to work. I've been complaining that my life is boring. This is the polar opposite of boring. And Jackson—holy hell, he's delicious. I can already taste him. What do I have to lose?

"Fuck it," I say. "I'm in."

He gives me that panty-melting smile again and I almost die.

"Perfect. Let's go."

7

MELISSA

"Wait, we're not leaving right this second, are we?" I ask.

He stands by the door, one hand on the doorknob. "Yeah. Why not?"

"I haven't packed or anything."

"Don't worry about it. Just grab your purse or whatever. You don't need anything else."

"But—"

"Melissa." His voice is soft, but there's an unmistakable air of command. The playfulness is suddenly gone and he's all business. "We're going. Right now."

I cast my eyes around, trying to think of anything I shouldn't forget. I'm mid-cycle, so hygiene products won't be necessary. I'm not on birth control, and my barren sex life over the last year means I don't have anything on hand. I'll have to make sure Jackson takes care of that, if that's where this is going.

Of course that's where this is going, dumbass. He's about to take you on a fucking sexcation!

I grab my purse, my phone, a light gray hoodie, and slip

sandals on my feet. I lock the door behind me and follow Jackson out to his car, feeling like I'm floating.

He holds the car door open for me. I sink into the seat and draw in a quick breath. It is literally the most comfortable thing I've ever felt in my entire life. Screw the sexcation, I can just sit in this car forever and never get out.

"This car is ... I don't know if I have the vocabulary," I say when he gets in on the driver's side.

"Yeah, it's sexy as fuck, isn't it? It's fast as hell, too, but I try to keep it mellow. I can probably outrun anyone on the road, but who needs that kind of drama? I think I'm the only person in the state who has one, so it's not like they wouldn't be able to track me down."

He points his phone at me and then types something.

"Are you tweeting this?"

"Yep," he says. "If you don't want me to show your face, I can crop it out. That's kind of hot, anyway. Makes you seem mysterious."

Before I can answer, he puts his phone down and starts the car. It purrs. It absolutely, motherfucking purrs. He pulls out onto the road and it feels like we're gliding across ice, rather than driving on pavement.

I start a text to Nicole. What do I even say to her? She'll kill me if I don't tell her, but she'll probably kill me for going. Before I finish typing, my phone *bing*s with a text from her.

Is that you in his car?

Is she stalking his Twitter feed? *Um, yes? How did you see that so fast?*

What do you mean, um, yes?

I laugh. *Yes, I'm in his car. He picked me up. I'll see you in a week.*

A week?!?!?!?!?! WTF, Melissa!

Overreact much?

It takes a minute for Nicole's next text to come, so I know it's going to be a good one. *I am NOT overreacting. Where are you going that you will be gone for a week? What do you even know about this guy? Are you sure you're okay? Do you know what you're doing?*

I don't know. Enough that I'm doing this. Yes, I'm sure. Maybe.

"Let me guess," Jackson says. "Sister, or best friend."

"Best friend. I don't have a sister."

"Tell her she has nothing to worry about. I'm going to take excellent care of you."

He says he's going to take excellent care of me and you have nothing to worry about.

You're insane. Fine, but we need a code word. If you're in trouble, just call or text and say cocker spaniel. That's how I'll know you need help.

I laugh out loud. Nicole is the sweetest. *Cocker spaniel? Really?*

Why else would you ever say that to me? It's perfect.

And she thinks I'm the one who's insane. *Okay, deal. Nic, don't worry about me. This is crazy, but I think I need a little crazy in my life right now. I'll text you all week.*

All right. If you're sure. Love you, girl.

Love you too.

I glance over at Jackson. His eyes stay on the road, his hands on the sleek steering wheel. Fancy hasn't ever been a big temptation for me, but even I have to admit this car is unreal.

"So, is this when you tell me where we're going?" I ask.

He doesn't answer, just turns the corners of his mouth up in a sly grin.

This is getting ridiculous. I know the point of this little

jaunt is to be spontaneous and a little bit crazy, but we hopped in his car without any luggage. Where is he taking me?

"Where have you already been? How much have you traveled?"

"Not much," I say with a shrug. "I went camping a lot as a kid. Nicole's family took us to Disneyland when we were twelve, and I went to Cabo with friends once in college."

"Good. That keeps our options open."

"Options? I thought you already knew where we're going."

"Honestly? I have no idea."

My mouth falls open. "Are you fucking serious?"

"Completely fucking serious."

Oh god, that voice. It's almost like he's growling at me. The man positively radiates sex, but he hasn't so much as touched me yet. The anticipation is killing me.

"So, what, we're just driving?"

"No, I know where we're going in the car," he says. "After that—well, that remains to be seen."

I have no idea what to say to that, so I watch out the window. I know we're heading north, but that could mean anything. What does he mean by *after that*?

For the next two hours, I try to ask questions, but he deftly deflects my attempts to find out more. We pull off at a town along the freeway to get lunch, and he takes a few pictures of me.

"You're a little Twitter-obsessed, you know that, right?"

"Yeah, my followers are going nuts," he says. "They're commenting with suggestions on where we should go."

"What, are you serious?" I think about opening Twitter on my phone, but it's too weird. I don't want to see what people are saying about us.

"Everyone wants to know who my mystery girl is," he says, flashing me that smile.

"The faceless girl. How lovely."

He just winks at me.

After lunch, we get back on the freeway and keep driving. We're less than an hour away from Seattle. I wonder if he'll take me to his house first. Where does a man like Jackson Bennett live? He said Queen Anne, which is one of the hill neighborhoods in Seattle. I don't know much about it—I've never lived in the city—but it must be nice. Judging by the car, it's probably a hell of a lot more than "nice."

"When did you move to Seattle?" I ask. If he won't tell me where we're going, maybe he'll tell me more about himself.

"After college. Mostly I moved out here to piss off my dad, but I loved it, so I stayed."

"What's he like?"

"My dad?" he asks. "He's a typical rich asshole. I don't talk to my parents very much."

"That's too bad."

"Not really. I take it you're close with your family, but we were never close, not even when I was a kid. I had nannies and went to boarding school."

Wow. That's ... kind of sad. "Brothers or sisters?"

"Okay, so we're doing the get-to-know-you thing. I have an older brother, Davis. He's the heir to the Bennett family throne. He works alongside my dad in Chicago. He's arguably a bigger asshole than my father. I have an older sister, too. Lindsay married some dude with old money and lives out in Boston. I haven't seen her in a few years."

"Wow, that's awful."

"Why?"

"I don't know. It's too bad that your family is so distant. I guess it's hard for me to relate. I don't have a big family—it was always just me and my dad—but we've always been close."

"What about your mom?"

I look down at my hands. It's hard to tell people about my mother. "She died when I was four."

"Oh, Melissa, I'm sorry." The concern in his voice is so genuine.

"No, it's okay. I mean, it *is* sad. But I don't remember her, or remember being sad about losing her. Not really. It was much harder on my dad."

"So your fisherman daddy raised you in Jetty Beach, all by himself."

"That he did."

"Is that why you still live there? To be close to your dad?"

"Partly," I say. "It's home."

"I've never had a place like that. I grew up in Chicago, but it never felt like home to me. I got out of there as soon as I could. I can't imagine going back."

"What about Seattle?"

"I like living there. What the fuck do I know? I have a penthouse condo with a view of the entire city. It's pretty amazing. I'd say that's a damn good home."

"I'm sure it's beautiful. Now will you tell me where we're going?"

"No."

My jaw drops when he takes the exit to the airport. The thought crossed my mind, but I dismissed the idea outright. He can't be taking me to get on a plane. We didn't bring anything with us. I have my ID on me, but only because I grabbed my purse. Other than that, I have a few bucks in cash, some lip gloss, a hair tie, and whatever miscellaneous things I left in my handbag over the last few months.

"Are we going to the airport?"

"Of course."

He doesn't take the exit to the main terminal, instead driving toward the off-site parking lots. He turns into the driveway of a tall building. It ends with a large, closed garage door. Jackson taps a few buttons on his phone, and the door opens.

He glides the car inside. It isn't a parking garage in the traditional sense. The floor looks more like marble than concrete. The finished walls are painted a soft beige, with art hanging in front of each parking spot. Jackson pulls the car into an empty spot—there are about a dozen all together, with two other cars parked further down. Nearby is a black limo with a driver in a suit standing next to it.

Jackson gets out, adjusting the cuffs of his shirt while he walks over to open my door. I'm not a fan of the whole door-opening thing some guys do—I can open a door for myself, thank you very much. But in this moment, I'm too dazed to even notice. I get up, remembering at the last second to grab my purse. Jackson puts a gentle hand on my back, his touch adding to my jitters.

The driver opens the limo door for me and Jackson guides me inside. He stands outside the door for a moment, talking to the driver. I don't hear what they say, but I see another man come out of a door off to the other side. Jackson talks to him too, and I think I see him slip him some money. A tip, I suppose.

I sink into the black leather seat. It's almost as comfortable as Jackson's car, but I don't think anything can compare to that. The L-shaped seat goes along the back and one side. The other side has a counter. A bottle of champagne sits in a silver bucket of ice and a dark wicker basket holds small, packaged snacks.

I wait while Jackson speaks to someone on his phone. My heart races. What is this? The last time I went to the airport, I parked at a cheap lot two miles away and a stinky ride-share van took me to the terminal.

"Sorry about that," he says, sliding into the seat next to me. The driver shuts the door and, seconds later, the car starts moving.

"That's okay, but ... what is all this?"

"Yeah, sorry, this isn't mine. This was the best they could do on short notice."

I stare at him, mouth wide open, while he checks something on his phone. A little voice in the back of my mind says I should text a picture of this insanity to Nicole, but I can't think straight.

The drive to the terminal is all of five minutes. Jackson gets out and pauses next to the open door. He offers me his hand and I let him help me out of the car. His hand feels strong and warm. It anchors me to some sort of reality—a reality that is quickly spinning out of control—and I don't want to let go.

"You ready?" he asks, his voice soft and low, as if we aren't standing in front of a crowded airport with cars rushing by.

"I think so."

With his hand on the small of my back, he guides me inside. His touch does nothing to ease my tension. His hand lingers, teasing just above my ass, first so light it almost tickles, then harder, his hand pressing into me with more authority.

"Let's see what we've got," he says. We walk up to the premium counter of one of the airlines. He pulls a card from his wallet and hands it to the ticket agent. "We need a flight."

The woman takes his card. "Of course, Mr. Bennett. Where are you traveling today?"

He looks at me and grins. "Where should we go?"

I probably look like some ditzy airhead, staring up at him like an idiot. "I ... I don't..."

He turns back to the woman. "What do you have leaving in ... " He looks at me again. "What, the next two hours? We don't want to wait around too long. Do you have a passport?"

I blink at him, then dig through my purse. I have a passport, but I don't carry it with me. Why the fuck would I need a passport on a regular basis? "No, not on me."

"Domestic, then," he says.

The ticket agent checks her computer, fingers tapping against the keys. "We have a flight to New York, with one layover in—"

"Direct only." He rubs his hand up and down my back. I don't want him to stop touching me.

"All right." Her eyes flick back and forth and she keeps typing. "There's a direct flight to Austin, Texas that leaves in ninety minutes. Kansas City, leaving in two hours. I have San Diego in seventy minutes, and Chicago leaving in three hours. That's all, Mr. Bennett. The rest are all booked."

"Hmm, not great options," he says. "What do you think?"

I open my mouth, but nothing comes out.

He pulls out his phone and taps a button, then puts it to his ear. "Tammi, what are my options in San Diego? I'm not thrilled about it, but I don't want to sit around at the airport, and there's a flight."

He pauses, listening.

"Good. Right, that place wasn't bad. The food was incredible. Is it available?" He waits, moving his hand from my back and putting it in his pocket. "Well, tell them they have to move. How many? Yeah, they can move. Tell them it's on me. Find them something else and I'll pay for the rest of their stay. Of course you did. This is why you're the best. Yeah, just take care of it. It's fine, I don't care about that. Perfect. Okay."

He hangs up, turns back to the ticket agent. "San Diego it is. Two."

8

JACKSON

Melissa and I take seats at a small table in the airline's executive lounge. The lights are dim and soft music plays in the background. She blinks at her surroundings, like she isn't sure how she got here. I check my messages while we wait for someone to take our drink orders.

"Good afternoon, Mr. Bennett." A young man in a shirt and tie stands next to the table. "What can I bring you?"

"Is it time for Scotch?"

Melissa nods. "It's definitely time for something."

"Glenlivet twenty-one, is that our favorite? Two. Straight up, with a splash of mineral water."

"Very good, Mr. Bennett."

"Did I get it right this time?" I ask.

"I'm impressed," she says. "It appears you can be taught."

Damn, I like her. Completely out of her element, her eyes as wide as a little kid at Disneyland, and she still has a saucy comeback.

This is definitely a good idea. I wasn't lying when I told

Melissa I have no plan. I woke up this morning and decided I was done flirting with her over fucking texts. I want her. I want her so bad I can already taste her.

At this point, I probably could have fucked her twice—once on her couch, and once in her bed—but I don't want it like that. I spent two agonizing weeks thinking about her, dreaming about her. She dug in, getting so deep under my skin I have no idea how to separate myself from her. I don't simply want sex. I want Melissa. I want to know what's going on behind those brown eyes, want her to tell me all her secrets with those sweet lips.

And sure, I want to impress her along the way. Sweep her off her feet. Do something crazy and unexpected. My assistant will need to juggle some things for me, but that's part of why I pay her so much money.

San Diego is hardly my first choice, but the villa where I'm taking her—it's worthy of Melissa Simon. She's going to love it. As far as the rest of it, I figure it doesn't matter where in the world we go. All I want is the chance to be with her—no distance, no interruptions.

I'm going to rock her world.

In the meantime, the anticipation is fucking delicious. I sip my Scotch, watching her. Her eyes move around the room, her finger circling the rim of her glass. She has that rare, effortless beauty, a look that's completely natural, and so alluring. I bet she looks amazing from the moment she wakes up in the morning. She'll linger in bed with me, letting me kiss her, touch her skin, run my fingers through her tangled hair. No getting up and rushing to the bathroom to put on makeup before I can see her. She's incredible. I can't take my eyes off her.

"Why are you staring at me?" she asks.

"Because you're beautiful."

The corners of her mouth turn up ever so slightly and she sips her Scotch. "You're crazy."

"A little bit."

I want to touch her again. Aside from putting a hand on her arm the first night we met, and helping her out of the car, I haven't felt her skin. I kept my hand on her back, only touching her through her clothes. I did it on purpose, waiting, keeping my hand just on the edge of how a lover would caress her. Familiar, safe, only hinting at what I have in store. Soon, I'll touch her skin again. I'm not sure if I'll do it now, or wait until we're on the plane. I want to draw it out, make every moment arousing.

Not that I need help there. The constant hard-on is getting a little uncomfortable. Every time I relax, I look at her or think about getting her to that villa, and I'm instantly hard again. Fuck, she is so tempting. Part of me wants to take her somewhere—now—and fuck her blind.

But this way is going to be so much better.

Her hand is on the table, her fingers just brushing her glass. I shift so my hand is near hers. I touch the backs of her fingers with the tips of mine, so light. Not too much. Not yet. My hand buzzes at the feel of her skin, and she draws in a quick breath. *Oh yeah, baby, I feel it too.*

I trail down to the back of her hand and she twitches. I get to her wrist and circle my fingers around it. So delicate. I turn her hand over, palm up, letting it rest in mine. With my other hand, I run a finger down each of hers, starting at the tip and stopping at her palm. I circle my finger around her palm, and her fingers curl up. I press my hand into hers, spreading her fingers, and rub up to her wrist. I let my fingers brush her forearm, then slide my hand back down, relishing the feel of her skin. It's better than it was in my mind, and my cock strains against my pants.

I think about bringing her fingers to my lips, but that will have to wait. I'm torturing myself, and hopefully her too, but I love it. This isn't my usual style. I usually get what I want, when I want it—I'm not very good at denying myself. But this is different. She's different. I don't want to move too fast and break the spell.

"Your flight is ready to board, Mr. Bennett."

I glance up at the waiter. "Thank you." I look back at Melissa. "Ready?"

We get right on the plane and settle into our seats, first class, first row. I never sit anywhere else. I don't like looking at the back of some asshole's head.

Melissa fastens her seatbelt and tucks her legs up. "I've never flown first class before."

I've never not flown first class. I don't even know what the back of a plane looks like. "If you have to fly commercial, it's the only way to go."

"Have to fly commercial? How else do you fly?"

"I charter a private plane more often than not," I say. "I don't own one. I've never bothered. Seems like too much hassle, so I charter when I need one. But for this little adventure, commercial seemed like the way to go. It adds to the spontaneity; don't you think?"

Her eyebrows draw together and her mouth hangs open. I can't wait to devour that sweet mouth. But not yet. Once I start, I won't be able to stop.

"You live a very strange life, Jackson Bennett."

"Do I?"

We sit while the rest of the passengers get on and the plane taxis to the runway. I fire off a tweet and send a few emails. Melissa watches out the window while we take off. When we get to cruising altitude, the flight attendant brings us drinks. Melissa tosses back her whiskey pretty fast. I order her another.

"Are you nervous on planes?" I ask. The flight took off without much turbulence, and so far everything has been smooth.

"No, not really. Today has just been such a whirlwind."

She sits leaning toward the window, resting her elbow on the opposite arm rest. Her drink is perched on her knee. Her hands are too far away for me to touch, but her feet... She let her sandals fall to the floor, and her feet are tucked up on the seat next to me.

I can't keep the grin off my face as I put my hand on her foot. I don't want to startle her, but she meets my eyes and laughs a little. Her toenails are painted bright green. I wrap my fingers around her foot and slide my hand toward her ankle. She shifts in her seat, stretching out her legs to put her feet in my lap. I rub my thumb around the ball of her ankle and she sucks in a quick breath.

This is going to be a long flight.

It's ridiculous how turned on I am, just by her feet. I'm not necessarily a foot guy. Everyone has their thing, and feet aren't mine—although I do love how a hot woman looks in a sexy pair of shoes.

Apparently I have a Melissa thing, because I want every bit of her. I clasp her foot with both hands and dig my thumbs into the arch, rubbing back and forth. Her eyelids flutter, and a slow smile crosses her face. I already love making her feel good. I want to see more of that face, feel that body relax against mine.

The flight goes on and we have more drinks. I find excuses to touch her—always her hands, her feet, or her arms. Nothing else. I'm saving the rest for later, and just knowing it's coming has me dying for the flight to be over. After a while, she leans closer to me and I play with her hand again, running my fingers up and down, tracing the lines on her palm. Her breathing is slow and even, and her head slips down to my shoulder. I rest my cheek on her head. I can't tell if she's asleep or just relaxed, but I let her be, still playing with her fingers and hand.

I drift off—which is weird, because I never sleep on planes. When the flight is over, we disembark—no need for baggage claim—and head outside. The sky is dark and headlights flash. I lead her to the car that's already waiting for us, and get in after her.

Melissa stares out the window as we drive to the villa. Neither of us say much on the way. We're both tired from traveling, and I'm a little buzzed from all the drinks on the plane. I send a few emails and check in with my assistant. Melissa hasn't so much as looked at her phone, but I figure she's just tired.

The car turns into the driveway and stops in front of the triple garage doors. I get out and go for Melissa's door, but she beats me to it. I'm disappointed we're arriving after dark—it's hard to see, and we're right on the beach. Still, we'll wake up to it in the morning.

A man in a white polo meets us out front. "Mr. Bennett," he says. "It's good to see you. I trust your flight was pleasant?"

I shake his hand, searching my memory. "Nathan. Is that right?"

"Yes, good memory," he says.

The last time I was here, Nathan was in charge of the villa. I remember him because he did such a good job, and he was personable without kissing my ass. I like him. "Thanks for getting things ready on short notice."

"Of course, Mr. Bennett."

Another man in a matching polo steps forward with a tray. "Champagne?"

I take one and hand it to Melissa. She blinks at me, but takes the drink.

"Thank you." I take one for myself and follow Nathan inside.

We walk in through a tiled foyer and up a short set of stairs. To one side is an expansive living room with floor-to-ceiling windows overlooking the ocean. A wet bar with a long granite countertop stands along one side, and a small staircase leads to another sitting area. More tall windows display the breathtaking view. The beige-and-blue furnishings are classic without being gaudy. I pause and survey the space. Tasteful. It will do.

"Your things have already been taken to your room," Nathan says.

"Our things?" Melissa asks, leaning toward me and pitching her voice low.

"I had some things sent over. I had to guess at your size, but it should get us through for now. We can go shopping for anything else you need tomorrow."

"The main living space is here," Nathan says, gesturing to the spacious room. "The kitchen is that way. Chef Louisa will be available daily to see to your meals. Downstairs is another living area with doors that open to the pool deck. From there, you'll find the staircase leading to the beach. I've set you up in the main master suite, but there are four other bedrooms to choose from. Feel free to select any one you'd like. Would you like the full tour, or shall I show you to your room?"

I look at Melissa. She looks awed, but there's a tightness in her eyes. "Thank you Nathan, I think we'll go to our room. This was a wonderful welcome. Thank you."

"Of course," Nathan says. "Would you like breakfast at nine?"

"Let's make it ten. We've had a long day. And I can find our room."

"Very good," Nathan says. "Good night."

"Good night."

Melissa doesn't say anything as I lead her upstairs to the master suite. We walk in and are greeted by the soft breeze coming off the water. Accordion doors open to a large balcony with a glass railing. The beach is just below. Two suitcases are in front of the king-sized bed, and a sitting area surrounds the gas fireplace. A door on the far side leads to a large bathroom. I can just see the tub and walk in shower. That could be interesting.

I dig in my pocket and toss my phone on the bed. I'll tweet a picture of the view in the morning, although even in the dark it's stunning. Moonlight glints off the water and the sound of the waves carries through the entire villa. I take a sip of my champagne and I'm about to invite Melissa out onto the balcony, when I see her face.

Something is wrong. Her forehead is tight, her eyes wide and glistening, and she holds a hand to her mouth.

"What's the matter?" I ask. "Don't you like it?"

She shakes her head slowly, her hand still covering her lips, the glass of champagne untouched in her other hand.

I move closer and pluck the drink from her hand, setting it on a side table. "Melissa. What's wrong?"

She drops her hand from her mouth and takes a deep breath. "You picked me up this morning in a car that I've never even heard of. I Googled it while we were waiting for the plane to take off. Jackson, that's a two-million-dollar car."

Was it that much? It probably was, but I can't remember.

"You can walk into an airport and say, 'Where should we go?' and then just … go. Your idea of slumming is flying first class. And this." She gestures around the room. "The house I grew up in would fit in this one room. The entire house. When you said we were flying somewhere, I thought … I don't know. I thought you'd book a Hilton or something. This is a fucking mansion. An entire village could live here, and it's just us."

She hasn't even seen the rest of it. If I recall, there's a movie theater downstairs.

"I don't know where I am right now," she says. "I just left town with a man I barely know, and he flew me to fucking San Diego with no luggage, and now I'm standing in a mansion on the beach, and I don't know what I'm doing here."

My shoulders slump. I didn't want to upset her. I thought she'd be ecstatic. I imagined her running out to the balcony, leaning out over the edge to see the beach below. We'd have a late night snack and get a little drunk. I could take my touching game from her ankles up her thighs, to her hips, her stomach, her breasts. But she isn't happy. She isn't relaxed and free, ready to let me explore her body.

I can fix this.

"Hey," I say, my tone soothing. "I'm sorry. This is my fault. I got this idea in my head and I charged forward without paying attention to you."

She hugs her arms around herself, her brown eyes so sad.

"Listen, you can have the room. There's another just down the hall. I can sleep there if you want. I won't push you into anything."

I don't want to leave her—the thought is so disappointing—but I never, ever force. A man who has to force a woman needs to examine what's wrong with him. I pick up my phone off the bed.

"Please don't leave."

Those words make my chest clench. "I won't leave you."

I glance around the room. There has to be a way to make her feel better. I grab an extra blanket out of a closet and bring it to her. "Come here," I say, wrapping the blanket around her shoulders. I lead her to the bed and ease her down. She sits and pulls the blanket tighter around herself. "Wait here. I'll be right back."

I run down to the kitchen. The staff all goes home at night, so I fumble around and find a serving tray. I search the fridge and bring out a bowl of strawberries, the stems already trimmed. The pantry yields a bag of tortilla chips and some salsa. I grab a couple bottles of water and, at the last second, decide to make her some tea. There's an instant-hot water tap at the sink, so I fill a mug and find some tea bags.

When I bring it all upstairs, I find her still on the bed. She wipes her eyes. Fuck, she's been crying. How the hell did this go so wrong? I set the tray on the bed, making sure the hot water won't spill, and sit down on the edge.

"This was the best I could do. I thought you might be hungry, since we missed dinner."

"Did you make me tea?"

"Well, there's hot water. I don't even know if you like tea."

"I love tea at night," she says, her voice soft.

I smile, meeting her eyes. God, she's beautiful. "Hey, I know what we should do. Let's see if this place has Netflix."

I grab a remote and turn on the TV. I settle onto the bed on the other side, careful to give her some space, and flip through the options.

"Can I tell you something I've never told anyone else?" I ask, giving her a little grin.

Her eyebrows lift. "Sure."

"I love *Firefly*."

She breaks out laughing. "You're kidding."

"I swear. It's my favorite show."

She laughs again. "You're fucking with me."

"No, I said I wouldn't fuck with you. It's a goddamn shame it was canceled, but at least he got to make the movie."

She shakes her head, looking at me with such disbelief. "I love *Firefly*, too."

"Yeah?"

"It's my favorite. I watch it whenever I'm stressed."

"Perfect. Here's what we're going to do. We'll eat our snack, and binge-watch *Firefly* until we fall asleep. Sound good?"

"Are you sure?" she says, clutching the mug in her hands. "I mean, you brought me here because—"

"Hey," I say, cutting her off. "I brought you here because I want to spend time with you." I let a grin spread across my face. "I'll make hot, crazy love to you later."

"All right, captain," she says with a small shake of her head. "Do it up."

9

MELISSA

My eyes flutter open and, for a second, I have no clue where I am. Soft sheets. The sound of the ocean.

Holy shit. I'm in San Diego. With Jackson.

I hold perfectly still, afraid to move. How did this happen? My heart beats uncomfortably hard. Jackson picked me up in a two-million-dollar car. He drove me to the airport, and put me on a plane. He brought me to a gorgeous mansion on the beach, the sort of place I imagine celebrities vacation. And when I flipped out on him, he made me tea and watched Netflix with me.

Who is this man?

He spent the entire trip touching me: my back, my hands, my feet. He never touched my face, nor did he try to kiss me. I wanted him to. I would have been happy to spend the plane ride making out with him in first class. I was anxious, but he was so confident and relaxed. And his hands felt so good. Every touch left me wanting more.

It was the mansion that broke me.

The car? Fine, he's rich, and rich men like flashy cars.

The ability to fly off at a moment's notice? That fits what I know of him. The car service, the first class, the nonchalant attitude like he has no idea how insane his life is? Fine. But it wasn't until he brought me to the villa that it hit me what he is.

Wealthy has always been an abstract concept to me. I grew up somewhere between poor and has-just-enough. My dad did the best he could, and we always had food on the table. I worked my way through college, which wasn't all that bad. I have a job and I own my little house. It isn't much, but it's mine. I have enough money to buy cute clothes once in a while, and help my dad pay his bills when he needs me.

Rich people are something that exist in movies. I've never given much thought to the sort of lives they lead. People with money are just people with more stuff, and they aren't particularly fascinating to me. I don't watch rich people reality TV, or dream home shows. So I didn't really know. I have no frame of reference.

I walked into this huge house—it's as big as an entire apartment building, and I know there are more floors downstairs—and I couldn't process it. I didn't understand what I was dealing with, but there it was, smacking me in the face with its insane view and expansive rooms.

And Jackson. I was so stunned, so completely taken aback, and he was nothing but sweet. I don't know why that surprises me. I guess I can't fathom that the cocky rich guy has such a compassionate side. *Firefly*? Really? We snacked and laughed and watched TV until we drifted off.

That was it.

I woke up in the night, still dressed, and decided to slip off my bra and jeans. After that, I slept like a fucking baby—at least, the kind that actually sleeps at night, because I'm told real ones don't. The bed is divine, the sheets so soft against my skin. Considering the circumstances, I wake up feeling fairly refreshed.

I face the edge of the bed, but I can feel Jackson's presence against my back. He isn't touching me—he didn't lay a hand on me all night—but it feels like his feet are close to mine. I hold my breath and hear the sound of his breathing, quiet and rhythmic. He must still be sleeping.

Risking a peek, I turn over and almost choke. He took his clothes off sometime in the night, and the sheet is down below his waist. His body is every bit as gorgeous as I thought it would be. It doesn't look real. Broad shoulders, muscular chest, and rippling abs. I can't tell if he's wearing underwear, or if he stripped down completely. I want to rub my hands all over that hot body, but all I can do is stare.

There's something about having shared a bed with him, dressed and without sex. It's so intimate. So sweet. I sort of assumed this week is all about getting in my pants. After our little sexting session the other day, it seemed like that's what he wanted. And looking at him now, I want him. Bad. I'm still half groggy, but my body stirs, and it wants Jackson Bennett.

My bladder, however, has other ideas.

I decide to slip out of bed while he's still sleeping, and use the bathroom. I feel gross, so a shower isn't a bad idea either. I peek in the bags he had delivered and find one that is clearly mine—the lavender dress is a giveaway. I bring it into the bathroom and quietly shut the door.

Whoever packed this did an amazing job. There's a little sundress, a tank top and shorts, a bag full of travel-sized toiletries, sunscreen, a hairbrush, and a blow dryer. Even a little satchel with nude-toned makeup. I can tell someone chose the panties with Jackson in mind—there are several pairs of lacy thongs. Everything has tags still attached, but is folded neatly in the bag.

The huge shower is tiled in a mosaic of ocean blue and copper. It's wide open, without a door. I get in and wash my hair. The hot water feels good, soothing more of last night's anxiety away.

"Good morning." Jackson's voice makes me jump. He holds the door open just enough to talk through, but doesn't come in.

"Hi."

"Do you have everything you need?"

"Yes, definitely." *Do you want to join me in the shower and let me lather soap all over that beautiful body?*

"Good. I'll let you do your thing."

The door clicks shut.

I let out a long breath and finish in the shower. After drying off, I choose the sundress. It fits perfectly, although it shows my bra straps more than I'd like. I decide to go for it and go braless. The dress hugs my chest enough, it holds the girls where they need to be. And it's way more comfortable.

I leave my hair wet and emerge into the bedroom. Jackson stands at the balcony, dressed in nothing but a pair of black boxer briefs, sipping coffee. Luckily I manage to pick my jaw up off the floor before he notices me.

He grins and puts down his mug. "Hey. Feel better?"

"Yes, a lot better. Thanks."

"Good."

"Sorry if I woke you earlier. I needed to wash the airplane off."

"No, it's fine."

He comes closer.

Keep your eyes up, Melissa. Keep your eyes up.

Too late. Oh my god, look how he fills out those underwear.

"Melissa?"

"Sorry, what?" Oh fuck, he said something and I was staring at his cock.

"The dress. It looks great. That was in the bag? Does everything fit?"

"Yes, perfectly." Even the little thong is surprisingly soft and comfortable.

"Great." He holds my eyes and all I can think about is whether I can get the thong off quickly enough. I'm hot and throbbing already.

"I think you had the right idea with that shower. Wash the plane off."

He sweeps past me, so close his skin almost brushes against mine. I think if it had, I would have jumped on him and wrapped my legs around his waist.

He goes into the bathroom, and as soon as he's out of sight I dive for my phone. It's about time I check in with Nicole. I think about texting her, but decide I need to call. I need to hear a real voice to make sure the plane didn't crash and I'm not actually dead.

"Oh my god, Melissa. Do you need to say the code word?" Nicole's voice is tinged with panic.

"There isn't much point to a code word if you have to ask if I'm going to say it." I'm pretty sure I can hear Ryan laughing in the background.

"Well, are you okay?"

"Yes, I'm fine."

"Where are you?"

I pause. "San Diego."

"What? I thought you were going to Seattle."

"Well, we went to the airport."

"Why didn't you tell me?"

"I didn't know. We went to the airport and picked a flight. It was ridiculous, Nicole. We flew first class. He drives a fucking two-million-dollar car. Who drives a two-million-dollar car?"

"He does?"

"Yes. And now we're in this mansion on the beach and I'm not sure I know what's happening." I glance over at the bathroom. Holy fuck, he left the door open. And if I lean, just so ... Yep. There he is. He has his back to me and water cascades down his perfect ass. He turns to grab something and—

Oh my god.

"Melissa?"

Fuck, I keep getting distracted by his cock. But holy shit, it's distracting.

"Yeah, sorry."

"You're okay, right?" she asks. "You want to be there with him?"

"Yes." I was freaked out last night, and I feel kind of stupid about it, but today I'm sure. I do want to be here, and only with him. "Yes, I'm good. This is ... fuck, Nicole, it's amazing."

"Okay, so how was last night, then?"

"Nothing actually happened last night."

"Seriously? You spent the night in a mansion on the beach with Jackson Bennett, and you guys, what, went to sleep? Did you sleep in the same room?"

"Yeah, we slept in the same bed, but he never touched me. I mean, he touched me all day yesterday, but nowhere naughty. Last night, though, I was so overwhelmed when we got here. So he wrapped me up in a blanket and made me tea."

"He made you *tea*?"

"Yeah. And we watched Netflix."

"Wow."

"Right? I know, this is insane."

"You know what you need to do, Melissa." I can tell by her tone she's going to tell me whether or not I want to hear it. "Go with it. You said you wanted a little crazy in your life. So get crazy. Take advantage. When will you ever have a chance like this again? Go wild. Have fun. Just be safe, okay?"

"I will. Promise."

"Good. I want you to show Jackson how to have the hottest sex of his life. Blow his mind."

I glance into the bathroom. Jackson is drying off in front of the mirror, running a towel over all that delicious muscle.

I laugh to hide the surge of lust that pours through me. "Okay, Nicole. I'll text you later."

I hang up the phone and put it on a table, then set my sights on Jackson.

10

JACKSON

"Hi."

I stop drying my hair and let the towel hang in front of me, just enough. I haven't put on any clothes yet—but I also didn't close the door. On purpose. I want to see what Melissa will do. If she's still skittish, we can go for a walk on the beach and come back for breakfast.

I woke up with the scent of her in my nose and I want her more than I've ever wanted anyone—or anything—in my life. But I'm not going to push. I'll let her come to me. I know it won't take long.

And come to me, she has.

She stands in the doorway, that hot little dress hugging her curves. Her nipples press against the fabric. She's stunning. The lines of her shoulders and arms are strong, showing just enough definition to make her look badass, but still feminine. Her wet hair hanging down is sexy as hell. I wonder if she'll let me pull it a little. Not too hard—I'm not into pain. But sometimes the line between pleasure and pain is thin. I'm good at pushing to the edge.

"Hey," I say.

"Feel better after your shower?" She leans against the door frame and licks her lips.

"Much."

I wrap the towel around my waist. I'm hard as a fucking rock, but I've held out this long. She hesitates, her eyes traveling up and down my body. This delayed gratification thing is way hotter than I thought it could be. I stare at her. Where should I begin? What will she like? How can I make her scream my name? The possibilities are endless.

Keeping one hand on the towel, I take a few steps toward her. She closes the distance, her face tilted up to mine. I haven't even kissed her yet. What happened to me? I slept all night next to a woman I want so badly I can taste it—and I haven't touched her. Yesterday I played with her hands and feet, teasing us both, but I haven't felt the softness of her lips.

"Thank you," she says, her voice almost a whisper.

I inch closer, brushing my nose against hers. "For what?"

"For bringing me here."

It's time. I smile and lean in, claiming her mouth with mine. Her lips part for my tongue and I push it in, unleashing some of the passion I've been holding inside. I slide my hand beneath her dress and grab her ass, pulling her against me. She moans. God, I love her noises. She wraps her arms around me, one hand on my neck, the other on my back just above the towel. Her breasts press against my chest.

I let the towel drop and leave her mouth, kissing down the side of her jaw, onto her neck. Her head tilts, her hair cascading down her back. I run my tongue up to her ear and nip her earlobe with my teeth.

Her hands find my cock and I groan as she grips it and squeezes. One hand runs down the shaft and the other plays with the tip. Her touch drives me crazy. With one hand still gripping her ass, I run the other up her body and cup her breast. I can't get enough of her.

She brings her hands to my chest and pushes—hard. I step away, suddenly confused, but she brushes the sides of my ribcage with her fingertips, as if to coax me closer.

Her hands trail down my abs and, licking her lips, she slowly lowers herself to her knees.

Oh, fuck yes.

Her mouth clamps down on my cock with a rush of heat and sensation. I lean my head back and close my eyes. She plunges down, then slides back up, her tongue licking the shaft, then circling the tip when she gets to the top. She takes it again, pulling in more of me than I thought she could take.

"Oh my god, Melissa, that feels amazing."

One hand runs around to my ass and she teases my balls with the other. Holy shit, this woman. She pulls up and sucks on the tip, then plunges down again. I fist my hand in her wet hair, guiding her. I enjoy the fuck out of every second, every movement, every little flick of her tongue. She's fearless, and it drives me crazy.

I feel her pull away and I let go of her hair. She puts her hands on my thighs and runs them up my hips, moving her mouth up my body. She kisses her way up my abs. My breath comes fast and my legs practically shake. I slide my arms around her as she stands, keeping her body close to mine.

Her mouth reaches my neck. I pull back and kiss her. My hands dig into her ass and I grind my cock against her body. She lifts onto her tiptoes, pressing herself into me, her arms tight around my neck.

I release the kiss and hoist her up. She wraps her legs

around my waist and I hold her, nothing but a slip of thong between my cock and her very hot pussy.

"Your turn," I say.

I carry her into the bedroom and lay her down on the bed. She starts to lift her dress but I lean down and grab her wrist.

"Wait. You have to wait until I tell you."

She smiles—a wicked, wicked smile—and stops.

I stand above her, my cock still slick from her mouth, absolutely aching to be inside her. Melissa holds herself up on her elbows and tips her legs apart, the hem of her dress sliding up her thighs.

"You have to be a good girl and do what I say. Can you do that?"

"No. I'm not a good girl."

I kneel on the bed and put my hands on her knees, pushing her legs back together. "No, Melissa. You have to do as you're told."

"Okay, captain. Tell me what to do."

Fuck, yes.

I slide my hands beneath her ass and tuck my fingers under her panties. She lifts her hips so I can pull them off. I toss them to the side and run my hands up the outsides of her thighs.

"Lie down."

She immediately obeys, that naughty twinkle still in her eye.

"Open your legs."

Her legs drop open. She's perfectly waxed, which is great news for me. I want my mouth all over that beautiful pussy. I run my hands down the insides of her thighs and she tilts her hips up.

"No, you have to wait."

I gently brush my fingers up her wet folds and she whimpers. Without warning, I slide two fingers inside her, pressing the heel of my hand into her clit. Her back arches and she moans again. I move my fingers in and out a few times, rubbing her clit in a rhythmic motion. Her hips rock up and down.

"Fuck, Jackson. How are you doing that?"

"You like that?"

"Oh my god, yes."

I pull my hand out and grip her thighs.

"No, don't stop."

"You don't get to tell me what to do, remember?"

Her head falls back against the bed.

I push her legs apart again and dive in. I run my tongue up one side, then the other. She tastes so sweet. I want it all. I press the flat of my tongue into her, rubbing up and down. She moves her hips and I keep going, grinding my tongue against her clit. Her legs open wider and I grab her ass. It's tight, her skin so smooth. I suck on her clit and she cries out.

Oh, yeah, that's what I want.

Her hands grip the sheets. I push my fingers in again, and don't let up with my tongue. She moans with every thrust. I love how loud she is.

I speed up and so does she. I can feel the heat of her climax building. I push her closer, my tongue relentless. She arches her back, rocking her hips into me.

"Oh fuck, Jackson!"

I stop, pulling away suddenly. Melissa takes heaving breaths and picks up her head to look at me. Her cheeks are flushed, her lips full.

"What? Why?" she asks between breaths.

"You don't have my permission to come yet."

"Oh my god."

"Turn over."

She takes two more breaths, then rolls over. "Jackson, we need protection. I'm not using anything."

"Up on your knees. I'll take care of it."

She lifts herself up to her knees and turns her head to look back at me. It's sexy as fuck. I reach for the nightstand where I slipped a packet of condoms. I'm certainly not unprepared. I pull one out of the package and slide it on.

"I hope you're ready for this," I say.

"You better fuck me hard, captain."

I'm supposed to be giving the orders, but in this case, I'm happy to comply.

I thrust my cock inside her, feeling her hot folds wrap around me. I groan; it feels so fucking good. I grab her hips and rock her back and forth, digging my cock into her pussy. I hit her hard with each thrust, and she calls out. I don't want to hurt her, but she takes it so deep, I give her what she wants. My orgasm builds too fast. I've wanted her for so long, stretching it out, letting the tension mount. And she's better than I imagined.

I stop, my cock plunged deep inside her, and hold her tight against me.

"Don't stop now," she says, breathless.

"Baby, you're too good. I'm going to come too fast." My cock throbs, but I want to make this last.

I pull out and grab her hips, turning her on her back.

"Dress off."

I help her pull her dress over her head. I pause for a moment, taking her all in.

"You're so beautiful."

Her eyes are dazed, unfocused. "Jackson."

I love hearing her say my name. "Say it again."

"Jackson."

She opens her legs for me and I lower myself on top of her. Her skin against mine feels unbelievable. I kiss her as I push my cock in again. My mouth lingers on hers, our tongues dancing, slow and luxurious. I move in and out, grinding up against her, listening to her soft moans each time.

I lift myself up and cup her breast. She moves with my thrusts, but I keep it gentle. Leaning down, I run my tongue around her hard nipple. She shudders and groans again. I flick it with my tongue, then take it in my mouth and suck. My other hand grabs her hip, moving her up and down my cock.

"Fuck, Jackson, don't stop."

I switch sides, tasting her other nipple. Her skin is soft and clean, her nipple a sweet little nub against my tongue. She moves her hips faster, urging me on.

"Melissa, you're incredible."

I can't hold back any longer. Nothing else exists. I thrust into her pussy, in and out, feeling her heat build. She calls out my name, over and over, each time making my blood burn. Her legs wrap around my waist and I push in deeper, fucking her hard.

"Yes, Jackson, fuck yes."

Her pussy clenches around me and it's too much. Spasms of pleasure overtake me. My cock pulses, each wave stronger than the last. Melissa's fingers dig into my skin and her back arches.

I feel the last of her climax as mine ends. I slump over her, breathing hard. My vision is blurry. I pick my head up and find her mouth, kissing her gently.

I pull out and roll off her, then deal with the condom. I'm still trying to catch my breath. She stays sprawled on her back, her arms above her head.

"Fuck, that was amazing," I say.

Melissa laughs and rolls toward me. I wrap my arm around her, drawing her in close. I'm spent, but I'm not ready to let her go.

She rests her head on my shoulder and drapes one leg over mine. I kiss her forehead. This woman. So strong. She knows exactly what she wants and isn't afraid to take it. She isn't afraid to give me what I want either.

Any fear I might have had that I built her up too far in my imagination is gone. She blew me away. I let my eyes drift closed, my fingers lightly caressing her skin.

This week is just beginning...

11

MELISSA

I lay sideways on the bed, my head on Jackson's shoulder, his arms wrapped around me. His fingers trace little circles on my arm and every so often he leans in and kisses my forehead.

He's nothing like I expected.

Granted, his body is as glorious as I thought it would be. All hard, sleek muscle that ripples and flexes. It's perfect. How a man can be endowed with that body, *and* that cock—it simply isn't fair to the rest of mankind. He stretched me in all the best ways, like he's made to fit inside me.

I was so hot for him, I knew an orgasm was a foregone conclusion, whether he worked to get me off or not. But he did. He wasn't a selfish lover. He touched me, teased me, used his fingers and his tongue—oh my god, his tongue. He wanted to make me feel good, like he enjoyed my pleasure as much as his own.

And the way he kissed me. So many men discount the power of the kiss. I love good sex—and I like it hard and a little rough—but his slow, sweet kisses were absolutely decadent. A new feeling creeps in around the edges and I try to shove it away. I'm not going to let anything ruin this moment. My body hums with contentment, Jackson is warm against me, and this is just the beginning of our week together.

He holds me close, his arms strong. Another surprise. He doesn't get up and get on with the day. He lingers. His breathing is even, but the way his fingers caress my skin, I know he isn't asleep. He doesn't try to fill the silence or grab his phone. He just holds me.

That feeling springs up again—the one I don't want to acknowledge. Suddenly, I want to get up. I want Jackson to snap a picture of me and tweet something, bragging about conquering @sassygirl555. I want him to make a phone call, and then gripe about stupid people. I want him to walk around with that swagger, toss out a credit card like it means nothing, and buy something expensive, just because he can.

Because this Jackson—this quiet, contented, affectionate Jackson—is suddenly too much for me.

I lift myself up, gently pushing his arms aside.

He gives me a lazy smile. "You don't have to get up. We can stay here as long as you want."

"Yeah, I just ... bathroom."

"Sure," he says, running a finger down my arm.

The way he looks at me makes my heart beat faster. He no longer looks like he's ready to devour me—his passionate hunger seems sated. But his eyes take me in and a smile crosses his face. He looks ... happy.

That shouldn't send me running for the bathroom, but it does. I close the door behind me and try to catch my breath. It's fine. I'm simply overwhelmed by the amazing sex we just had. And let's not forget that I'm in a mansion on the beach, the sound of the waves carrying through the walls.

This is good. I can do this.

. . .

After breakfast—some of the best food I've ever had, I shit you not—we wander down to the beach. I wear the lavender sun dress and carry my sandals in my hand, feeling the sand beneath my feet. Jackson is dressed casually, in a blue t-shirt and long shorts, a pair of sleek sunglasses on his face. The waves run up and down the beach. I put my feet in the water, letting it splash against my calves. It's pleasantly warm—I've never felt anything like it. I grew up on the beach, and it's the same ocean, but this is nothing like the ice-cold water I'm used to.

Jackson never stops touching me. He holds my hand, rubs my back, runs his fingers down my bare arms. He pauses behind me, threads his arms around my waist, and leans down to kiss my neck. He takes pictures—mostly me, but a couple selfies of both of us—and tweets a few. My phone is in my purse, but I'm not sure I want to see what he's tweeting anyway.

What is he saying about me? I'm just his latest diversion, and building me up as some kind of mystery is probably fun for him. I let it go. I knew what I was getting into, and being the object of his followers' fascination is part of the deal.

Twice I notice people taking pictures of us. They make no attempt to conceal what they are doing—just walk closer, hold up their phones, and point them at us as we walk by. Jackson doesn't say a word, but deftly puts himself between me and the gawkers, a protective arm around me. We don't walk much farther before he mutters something under his breath about idiots with cameras, and turns me around so fast I almost trip.

We go back to the villa, and he calls for a car so we can do some shopping. We both need more clothes. A driver arrives in a black limo and holds the door open for us. Jackson plays with my hair and kisses my fingers as we drive.

The car pulls to a stop and he moves away. I take a deep breath, blinking hard. His touch leaves me feeling dazed, and it takes me a second to remember where I am. The driver lets us out at a large open-air mall, the walkways lined with palm trees. Jackson tips him and slips on his sunglasses.

We walk past a few stores, and I try not to stare. Some have names I recognize—Coach, Burberry, Gucci—but I've never been in any of them. Others look just as designer, but I'm so out of my element, I don't even know what they are. Jackson walks next to me, his hands in his pockets. He might as well have a sign on his chest that says *Rich as fuck*. He doesn't do anything to flaunt it. But the way he carries himself—the way he walks, the way his sunglasses fit his face like they're custom made, the way his clothes drape off his ridiculous body—make him look like he has a halo of money surrounding him.

Other people notice him, too. Heads turn; men stare at him as much as women. He glances in the windows of a few stores before he seems to decide on one. He holds open the door for me, and I walk in.

Men's clothing takes up one half of the store, women's clothing the other. I'm used to places that fill the floor with racks of clothes, using up every inch of retail space. This is positively empty by comparison. The walls and floor are soft beige, and two dark wood doors stand along one side—dressing rooms.

Mannequins display beautifully put together outfits, and the racks of clothing are spaced well apart. A stunning woman with long, dark hair and olive skin stands behind a small counter. She wears an impeccable white blouse, her lips a deep shade of red.

Jackson doesn't so much as look at the clothing on the racks. He walks up to the woman, leans his elbow against the counter, and takes off his sunglasses.

"I need six or seven shirts and pairs of shorts, and throw in a few pairs of slacks." He pulls out his wallet and plunks down a card. "And whatever she wants."

The woman glances at the card and smiles. "Of course, Mr. Bennett."

I stare at the clothes. The lack of selection is paralyzing. When I shop, I go straight for the sale racks and dig. You always find the best deals tucked in with the wrong size—the little treasures other people miss. I clasp my hands together and blink like an idiot.

The woman appears next to me, all smiles and white teeth. "What would you like to see?"

I have no idea. Jackson still leans against the counter, flicking his thumb across his phone.

"How about I bring you a few things to try?" the woman says.

"Um, sure."

I know Jackson isn't worried about the money, but I don't want him to have to buy everything for me. This is a high end store, but surely I can pay for my own clothes. It isn't like I have any other expenses this week.

I wander over to a rack with a few flowing peach-colored tank tops. I grab the tag to look at the price, and almost choke. Four hundred seventy-five dollars? What in the actual fuck?

Jackson looks up at me. My bewilderment must show because his eyebrows draw in with a look of concern. He walks over to me and put a hand on my arm. "Are you okay?"

"No, I am not okay. This shirt is almost five hundred dollars. My first apartment didn't cost this much."

He looks around as if he has no idea what I mean—and he probably doesn't. "Do you want to go somewhere else? I'm sorry, I just always shop here."

"I..." My voice trails off. How can I buy clothes in a place like this? I can't even afford one stupid tank top. Why did he bring me here?

He squeezes my arm. "Don't worry about it. I'll take care of everything."

He walks to the back of the store where the woman is draping clothes over one arm. They speak quietly for a minute or two and she nods along. He comes back, a triumphant smile on his face.

"There," he says. "She'll send what we need to the villa. You don't have to do anything. I had her send more than we need, so if you don't like anything, you can just leave it."

I gape at him. I feel like I do that a lot, but I can't help it.

He puts his sunglasses back on and clasps my hand, leading me out of the store. "I'm hungry," he says once we're outside. "Are you hungry?"

"Starving, actually." I let out a breath, trying to clear my head. Lunch. That's something I can handle—and pay for. "Let me pick the restaurant though."

"Sure. What sounds good?"

I have no idea what else is nearby, but I spotted a Cheesecake Factory when we first arrived. I'm sure that isn't a Jackson sort of restaurant, but it's perfect. I desperately need something normal. I lead him across the way, veering toward the bright red sign.

"Cheesecake?" he asks. "Don't we need lunch?"

I laugh. "They have lunch. They have a huge menu, actually. I'm sure you'll find something."

He shrugs and puts a hand on my back. "All right, if this is what you want."

We go in and a waitress seats us at a booth. The hum of conversation buzzes around us.

"This menu is like a book," he says.

"I told you."

He thumbs through the pages, looking skeptical.

"You've really never eaten at a Cheesecake Factory?"

"No. I've heard of it, but I thought, you know, cheesecake. I hate cheesecake."

I don't know why I find that so funny, but I can't stop laughing.

He lets his menu drop to the table and grins. "You're laughing at me."

"No," I say, shaking my head. "Okay, yes."

"All right, sassy girl."

A waitress comes and takes our orders. I order a burger with fries and one of the beers they have on tap. Jackson doesn't look at the menu again, just tells the waitress he'll have whatever I ordered.

Our food comes and we chat as we eat. Jackson doesn't seem to mind the meal, and the beer is good. When we finish, the waitress brings the check.

Jackson reaches for his wallet, but I snatch the folder with the bill sticking out of the top. "This was my choice, so I'm buying lunch."

"Don't be silly." He reaches across the table.

"Nope," I say, holding the folder out of his reach. I pull my debit card out of my wallet and stick it inside, then set the folder on the table.

The waitress walks by and takes the check.

"Melissa, you don't have to do that."

"No, but I can, so I want to."

He shrugs and looks at his phone. I think about texting Nicole, but the waitress returns. She holds out the folder, a tense look on her face.

"I'm sorry miss, but your card was declined."

I die. Right there, in a booth at the Cheesecake Factory. Dead.

My stomach turns over and I grab the folder. "Are you sure? That can't be right." There is no way. I have money in my bank account. I know I do.

"Here," Jackson says, reaching for the bill.

"No." I put it down and fumble through my purse. Did I give her the wrong card?

"It's all right," Jackson says. He hands the waitress his credit card and she walks away.

"What the fuck, Jackson?"

"It's just lunch. Don't worry about it."

It *isn't* just lunch, and I *am* worried about it. I'm so embarrassed, I want to crawl under the table. "I said I'd pay for lunch. I have money, I don't know what's going on. I have to call my bank."

"Really, Melissa, I don't mind."

"That's not the point." I'm too angry to sit here while he pays for our lunch, so I get up and storm out of the restaurant. Tears sting my eyes. Fuck, this is not going to make me cry. I stop outside the doors and pull up the banking app on my phone. I log in and look at my balance. I still have five hundred dollars in checking, plenty more in savings, and I know my bills are paid. Why did they decline my card?

I'm so mortified. He probably thinks I have no money. Of all the times to have my debit card fail, it has to be in front of Jackson Bennett.

He comes out of the restaurant and walks toward me, slowly, like he isn't sure of himself. "Hey."

"I have money in my account. I don't know why that happened."

"Of course you do. But if you didn't—"

"No." I stop him before he can say more. Plane tickets, villas on the beach, clothes that are so expensive I'll be afraid to wear them—all of that is bad enough. He is not going to suggest giving me money. "Don't even go there."

He holds up his hands. "All right. I just mean you don't have to worry about anything this week. I'll take care of it. I want to."

I know he does, but the embarrassment stings. I don't want to be his little charity case. I take care of myself just fine. "Let's just go."

Jackson nods and pulls out his phone to call the driver.

12

MELISSA

Jackson tries to get handsy with me in the limo, but I keep my distance. I don't want any more games. If he takes my picture again, I'll probably slap him, but he's smart enough to leave that alone. When we pull into the driveway, I throw open the car door myself and get out before the driver can come around. Nathan is there to let us in, asking about dinner, but I sweep past him and go upstairs to the bedroom. I run into the bathroom and bang the door shut, pressing the lock.

The bathroom doesn't help. It's too perfect. Too beautiful. The finishes shine, and the towels are so thick and soft. I wet a washcloth and put it on the back of my neck, trying to calm down.

What else did I expect? That a fucking gazillionaire would take me on some crazy vacation and expect me to pay for half?

I take a deep breath and put down the washcloth. I freaked out again, and it isn't Jackson's fault. It's not like he knows any better. He can't possibly understand.

I come out of the bathroom to find him on the balcony,

talking on his phone. His eyebrows are drawn down, his face serious. He lifts his eyes, noticing me, and says a few more words, nodding as he talks. He hangs up and pockets his phone.

"Melissa, I didn't mean to upset you."

"I know. I was just embarrassed. I'm sorry I was such a bitch about it."

He smiles, his lips parting over his perfect teeth. "You weren't. Are you okay now? Do we need to watch *Firefly* again?"

I laugh and step closer. He draws me in close, putting his arms around me, and kisses the top of my head. I close my eyes, savoring the feel of his body next to mine, his arms wrapped around me.

THE NEXT FEW days go by in a blur. We eat amazing food, lounge by the pool, walk on the beach. Now that we have plenty of clothes to wear, and there's a chef to prepare our meals, there doesn't seem to be any reason to leave the villa. It's our own little private paradise.

We take naps entwined in each other's arms, and stay up late decimating the villa's well-stocked bar. In the mornings, we nurse our hangovers with coffee and gourmet breakfasts. The sun shines and the skies are clear. Jackson takes a few work calls, and occasionally spends time on his phone answering emails. I check in with Nicole, assuring her I'm having a great time.

By Thursday, I'm trying very hard not to think about the approaching weekend. He hasn't mentioned when we're leaving, but we said a week. That probably means Saturday. I don't know if he made flight reservations, and I can't bring myself to ask. I don't want to think about this week ending. Jackson is fun and sexy as hell. He seems to enjoy being with me as much as I enjoy being with him. I want to relish the time we have left, instead of dwelling on what will come next.

Because I have no idea what *next* is going to look like.

That afternoon, we meander down to the beach. I wear a mint-green tank top and a flowing skirt that just hits my knees, my feet bare. The sun beats down, but a cool breeze blows in off the water. With all the time we spend outside, I'm getting a great tan.

We stop in front of the water and Jackson stands behind me, his hands running up and down my bare arms.

"This is amazing," I say. "I'm going to go ahead and bust out a cliché, because it's true. I feel like I'm living in a dream."

"Yeah, it's good."

There's something in his voice. Hesitance? I glance up at him, but he smiles, nothing unusual in his eyes.

He runs his hands through my hair and massages my scalp with his fingers. I let out a long, slow breath and lean my head back. He moves his thumbs up and down the back of my neck, pressing softly.

"That feels so good," I say.

"Mm, I love making you feel good."

He rubs my shoulders and I close my eyes. I feel like I can do this forever.

Don't think about forever.

One hand slides around my waist, pulling me against him. The other lifts the side of my skirt, his fingers trailing up my outer thigh.

His mouth is right next to my ear and he speaks in a throaty whisper. "We should go inside."

"We definitely should."

We walk back toward the villa, Jackson's hands all over me. He follows me up the stairs to the pool deck, grabbing my hips. When we get to the glass door leading inside, he spins me around and pushes me up against it. He grabs my wrists and raises my arms over my head, pinning me with one hand. His other hand reaches beneath my dress and pushes my thighs apart. He slides his fingers inside, his eyes locked on mine.

"You're wet again."

"What are you going to do about it, captain?"

"I'm going to fuck you until you beg for mercy."

His fingers do their magic and he leans down to kiss me, his tongue firm and aggressive. I lift one leg, half wrapping it around him, and he keeps my hands pinned above my head.

The sound of voices comes from somewhere nearby. He pulls his mouth from mine.

"I think someone's coming," I whisper.

His lips part in a sly smile. "We should go in." He tightens his grip on my wrists and presses his thumb against my clit.

My eyes roll back. "Oh fuck, Jackson. We need to go inside."

He curls his fingers and rubs in slow circles, that devil smile on his face. "Now?"

"Yes, now. I want it hard. You need to stop holding back with me."

He pauses, his face close to mine. "I don't want to break you."

"You won't. I'll stop you if it's too much."

He gently bites my lower lip as he slides his fingers out and lets my arms go. My whole body is on fire, my heart beating out of my chest.

Somehow we get the door open and stumble into the villa. We make our way to the master bedroom and he shuts the door. I back up toward the bed, Jackson right in front of me, almost pushing me backward. He pulls off his shirt and tosses it aside. My legs hit the bed and he stops, his gaze intense.

"Do you trust me?" he asks.

My heart flutters. His question is saturated with meaning, and I'm almost afraid to answer.

"Yes."

"Are you sure?" The seriousness in his face eases as one side of his mouth turns up in a smile.

He's never given me a reason not to. "Yes."

He digs into his suitcase and pulls out two neckties.

Holy shit.

His eyes don't leave my face as he walks back to me, the ties dangling from his hands. I take a trembling breath. I know what he's going to do. I've never done anything like this before.

I can't wait.

He puts the ties on the bed and helps me undress. I stand in front of him, naked and quivering with anticipation. He knots a loop in one of the ties and slips it over my wrist, then does the same for the other.

"On the bed."

I don't even consider resisting. I get on the bed, letting him guide me where he wants. I lay on my back and he straddles over the top of me. He raises my arms above my head and fastens the neckties to the bedframe, running a finger between the tie and my wrists, as if to make sure they aren't too tight.

"Stay here."

I swallow hard. He gets up off the bed and leaves the room.

I stare at the ceiling, my thoughts running a million miles a second. I'm completely in his power—and it's thrilling. The ties are loose enough that I can probably get free if I want to. But not knowing what he's going to do with me makes my adrenaline pump. I wait, squashing the urge to squirm against the restraints. Where is he?

What is he going to do?

He comes back in carrying an amber bottle and two glasses.

"We drank all the Glenlivet." He sits down on the edge of the bed and puts the bottle and glasses on the nightstand. "But this should do."

I watch him in a daze as he pours a splash of Scotch into one of the glasses. He picks it up and gently sets it just below my belly button.

"Hold still, or you'll spill your drink."

Fucking hell, that's just mean.

He pulls off the rest of his clothes and climbs on the bed. The Scotch sloshes back and forth in the glass.

"Careful," he says.

He tilts my legs open and runs his hands down my thighs, then teases his fingers along my folds. I watch him, trying to hold my body still.

"Oh god, Jackson."

"Baby, I love hearing you say my name."

He massages my clit—he's become an expert in just a few days—and I lean my head back against the pillow. I start to move my hips but he stops.

"Don't spill."

I groan. He rubs again, slipping his fingers inside and

using his thumb. He touches me with sensual slowness, and my eyes roll back.

"God, Jackson, that's so good."

I look up at him again. His mouth is turned up in a mischievous smile, his cock hard.

"Touch yourself while you do that."

He lifts one eyebrow. "You dirty, dirty girl."

"Do it."

He switches hands and rubs some of my wetness across the tip and down his shaft. His hand grips his swollen cock, rubbing up and down to the slow rhythm of his thumb on my clit.

"Holy shit, Melissa."

"Faster."

I never thought watching a man rub his own cock would be so fucking hot, but it makes me absolutely burn for him. He speeds up, and the glass tilts back and forth. I don't give two shits if it spills all over the bed. There are others. We don't have to sleep here.

"Woah, baby, slow down." He stops and pulls his fingers out. "God, Melissa, you're too much. Where did you come from?"

"You better put that cock in me soon before I have to take care of things myself."

He smiles his wicked grin. "You can't. You're all tied up."

I pull against the restraints and the glass tips. Jackson catches it before it spills.

"Bad sassy girl. You almost spilled your drink."

He tilts the glass just above my stomach and lets a dribble of Scotch pour out over my skin. He leans down and licks it off, running his tongue up my belly.

"I've wanted to do this to you since the first night we

met." He splashes more Scotch over the hollow of my belly button and purses his lips to suck it off.

"You thought about drinking Scotch off me when we were at Danny's bar?"

He dribbles more between my breasts and licks it, his tongue sliding across my nipple.

"Fuck yeah, I did."

I shudder and moan while his tongue makes lazy circles across my skin. "Did you think you'd get the chance?"

He stops and looks up, meeting my eyes. "Yes."

He puts the glass aside and unfastens the neckties from the bed frame, then ties them together, keeping my wrists shackled. He pulls me to the side of the bed and turns me on my belly. I'm face down, my legs bent over the side of the bed, my feet on the floor. I hear the crinkle of the condom wrapper and seconds later, he rams himself in. No waiting, no teasing. He pounds me hard. I cry out with each thrust. With my wrists tied together, I'm completely in his control.

I fucking love it.

There's nothing I can do but grind my hips into him as he pounds me fast. I told him what I wanted, and he's giving it to me. Every thrust is an explosion of ecstasy. I pick myself up onto my elbows and he reaches around to cup my breasts, never slowing.

"Jackson!" I practically scream. In the back of my mind, it occurs to me that the villa has a staff and they're probably around, but I don't care. How does he *do* that? Most men have to fumble around with each new position until they get it right—and most never do. Jackson *knows*. My vision goes blurry and I call out his name. God, it's amazing.

He grabs my hips and thrusts in harder. It hurts a little. My breath catches in my throat, and I feel a twinge of fear.

Am I safe with him? Will he stop if I need him to? How far can I let this go?

"Jackson, stop."

Instantly, he stops moving. No hesitation, no finishing what he's about to do. He stands motionless, his tight grip on my hips easing.

I turn my head to look at him. His chest glistens and he breathes fast.

"Did I hurt you?"

"No."

He pulls out and turns me over. We climb back onto the bed and he gets on top of me, pushing my arms above my head. He holds himself up, our bodies close. He slides his cock back inside and pauses, his face next to mine.

"Are you all right?"

Tears spring to my eyes at his sudden gentleness. He didn't do anything I didn't ask for—didn't want. "Yes, I'm fine," I whisper. "I just had to know I was safe."

He kisses my lips, his mouth so soft. "You're always safe with me."

With his lips on mine, he slides his cock in and out, pushing against me with each movement. He eases into a gentle rhythm. I grab his ass and move him faster, rocking my hips against him. He breaks the kiss and looks at me.

"Fuck me harder, Jackson."

He picks up the pace.

"Harder."

He does what I ask and my orgasm builds—fast. My muscles clench and my pussy throbs.

"Oh god, don't stop that."

"Fuck, Melissa, you feel so good. I can't stop."

He keeps going, harder and faster. I cry out as he brings me to the brink. His cock pulses inside me and I lose control. I call his name, over and over, while spasms of pleasure rip through me.

We both finish and he leans down, brushing his cheek against mine. He kisses my ear, down my neck.

"That was unbelievable," he says, his voice a low whisper.

It was. The entire week has been unbelievable.

I don't want to wake up.

13

JACKSON

The couch is damn comfortable. I sit, sprawled out on the cushions, a glass of bourbon resting on my knee. Melissa sits on the other side, facing me, her feet tangled with mine. We've been drinking since lunch and I'm buzzing pretty hard. A bank of clouds rolled in this morning, obscuring the sun, but the view from the huge windows is still stunning. Not as stunning as the woman rubbing her toes against the bottoms of my feet, but close.

I'm still dazed from the day before. Drinking Scotch off her skin was hot as fuck. As was her suggestion to rub my own cock in front of her.

I know I have a reputation, but half of it is just show. But, Melissa. This schoolteacher from some random town on the coast. She's a little bit dirty with a side of sweet and I can't get enough of her.

When I have to take work calls, I stay close, not wanting to be too far from her. I don't make up excuses to leave for a while, just to get some space. Usually spending this much time with a woman will start to irritate me. I'll notice her flaws, her annoying habits. Her voice will grate on my nerves and I'll want to get away. But not this woman. Not my Melissa.

A thought runs through my head, almost killing my buzz. Our flight home leaves tomorrow. We said a week, and we'll go back to our own lives. I'll take her home. No strings. No expectations. And that should be fine. That's exactly what I wanted.

But the thought of this ending opens a space in my chest—makes me feel like I can't quite breathe.

I down the rest of my drink in one swallow. Fuck that noise. We need to have some fun.

"I have an idea," I say.

Melissa's eyebrows lift. "Uh oh. Should I be scared?"

"Maybe."

"Then tell me."

I grin. "I want to take you dancing."

Her eyes widen and her lips part. "You dance?"

"Of course I dance."

"You're shitting me."

I laugh. "No, I'm serious."

"If you can really dance, I'm going to rip off your pants and suck your cock right this second."

"Fuck, I love your dirty mouth."

Melissa giggles, almost spilling her drink in her lap. "Okay, captain. Take me dancing. But I have no idea what to wear."

I meet her eyes. "Will you let me buy you something sexy? I want to dress you up."

She purses her lips like she's trying not to smile.

"Come on," I say, nudging her feet with mine. "Little black dress. Sexy heels."

"I don't do heels."

"They don't have to be super high to be hot. Besides, I'm told comfortable heels exist. I bet we can find some Jimmy Choos that are amazing. Or maybe something in a kitten heel. They're not so high."

"Kitten heels? How the fuck do you know what that means?"

"I like shoes."

Her mouth drops open. "I've been walking around here barefoot this entire time, and *now* you tell me you like shoes?"

"You have so many other things I like, I haven't even thought about your shoes."

She narrows her eyes. "If I didn't know better, I'd wonder if you're straight."

I grin. "I like the way shoes look on women. There's a difference. Let's do it. This will be fun, I promise."

She rolls her eyes. "Fine."

I take her to Jimmy Choo and talk her into a pair of peep toe pumps in champagne glitter. They look positively delicious on her little feet, and she admits they are comfortable. I almost decide to say the hell with going out, and bring her back to the villa so I can fuck her with those shoes on. But I want to get out.

I can't deal with the inevitable quiet. I have to do something to distract myself.

And I can fuck her with the shoes on later.

I find her a dress at Neiman Marcus, a one-shoulder sheath dress that hugs her curves beautifully. It's simple and classy—perfect for Melissa. I buy myself a new dress shirt, and an Armani jacket and slacks—Armani makes my ass look good.

Because I'm on a roll, and she isn't saying no, I take her to a salon. One stylist does her hair, while another does her makeup. She doesn't look too uncomfortable, although we're both a little drunk. I sit watching her, a stupid grin plastered to my face, while a guy with bleached-blond hair gives me a trim.

We go back to the villa to change. I finish first, so I lean against the front door, flipping through things on my phone.

Melissa comes out and I almost drop my phone. She is ... unbelievable. There is no other word. That dress, those shoes, her hair blown out, just enough makeup to enhance her eyes and lips. She rolls her eyes and slides her hands along the dress, as if to smooth it out.

"This is what I'm talking about," I say. "Do you have any idea how gorgeous you are?"

"No."

"That is a damn fucking shame." I take a few pictures of her with my phone.

"Bragging to your followers?"

"Nope," I say, thumbing through the pictures. "These are only for me."

The driver takes us north to Addison, a restaurant I've been to once before. From there, it's half an hour's drive to the Gaslamp Quarter where I want to take Melissa later, but it's early enough in the evening that we have time for a leisurely dinner. Addison doesn't disappoint. I order the chef's tasting menu and let the staff choose the wine. The French-inspired cuisine is delicious, and the staff discreet and professional. Melissa claims it's the best meal she's ever eaten.

We linger at Addison, sipping wine, until well after the sun goes down. Eventually, we go back to the car and head to the Gaslamp Quarter. I kiss her neck and nibble on her fingers as we drive.

The car pulls to a stop and the driver opens the door. I get out of the car, adjust my jacket and hold out a hand for Melissa. Her sexy little shoes come first, followed by those luscious legs. She stands and gives me a little smile. I put a hand on the small of her back and lead her toward the bouncer at the front of the club.

"There's a line," Melissa says, gesturing toward the mass of people stretched down the side of the street. Parq always has a line.

One corner of my mouth turns up. "I don't do lines."

I approach the bouncer, a muscular man with a thick beard and tattoos down his arms, and ignore the scowls of a few girls in gaudy makeup at the front of the line.

"Sir?" the bouncer asks.

I put one hand in my pocket and keep the other on Melissa's back. "Jackson Bennett."

The bouncer blinks, his face showing recognition, and unhooks the rope to let us in. "Have a nice evening, Mr. Bennett."

I smile at the girls in line as I walk by, and pause long enough to let someone behind them take my picture.

"How do you do that?" Melissa asks.

"Do what?"

"That. Normal people don't just walk up to a bouncer and give their name. People treat you like royalty."

"They treat me like I have money. Bouncers want people inside that the people outside will talk about."

"I guess that means they want you."

"Exactly. They always want me."

We walk in through the outer lobby and a man in a gray suit appears. "Mr. Bennett, thank you for coming to Parq.

We have the owner's booth ready for you. Are you expecting any more personal guests?"

"No, just us tonight."

"Perfect, this way."

Maybe it's the day's constant stream of bourbon and wine, or maybe Melissa is getting used to being with me, but she moves with confidence, her hand tucked in the crook of my arm.

Music pulses, the noise level rising as we make our way up a ramp to the main club. The light show is in full swing, colored beams racing around the room. Women in white bikinis dance on elevated platforms, and guys in seven-foot robot costumes walk the floor.

Our host brings us to our booth. The bottle service girl isn't far behind, dressed in a black bodysuit with a plunging neckline that barely covers her enormous implants. I order our drinks and watch as a train of girls with sparklers prances by. People fill the dance floor and curious onlookers wander near our booth, trying to get a look at us. The host stands at the entrance and keeps the gawkers back.

I do the club a favor and snap a picture of Melissa, her face turned away from me, and tweet where we are—*Sassy Friday night at Parq San Diego*—and add a few hashtags. I scroll through some of the replies on my earlier tweets. Most are pretty standard. People are dying to know about Melissa—who she is, where we are. Tonight they'll want to know what she's wearing. I take a picture of her shoes, showing off the sexy curve of her legs. *The dress might have to come off, but the Jimmy Choos will stay on.*

Some asshole replied to another tweet with a comment about fucking Sassy Girl when I'm done with her. I block him. The Internet is full of jackasses. They aren't worth my time.

The bottle service girl pours shots and I hand one to Melissa. My buzz is starting to wear off and I want to get another drink down before my mind clears too much.

"What should we drink to?" I ask.

"To a crazy end to a crazy week."

I fucking hate that toast. I look away for a moment, trying to ignore the pain that stabs through my chest. I lift my glass. "Let's just drink to crazy."

"To crazy," she says and downs her shot.

I swallow mine and glance at the bottle, wondering if I should have another. But it isn't even midnight, and I never drink enough in public to make an ass of myself. I lounge back against the cushioned seat, my arm behind Melissa.

A small knot of women lingers near the booth, giggling and pointing at me. Our host keeps them back, but one leans over the barrier.

"Jackson! Jackson Bennett! Let us party with you!"

"Please," another one calls. She runs a finger down her neck to her cleavage, her boobs barely contained by her neon orange top.

Our host meets my eyes and I give him a small shake of my head.

"Move along, ladies," he says, holding up a hand to push them back.

Melissa laughs and drapes her legs across my lap, her feet crossed at the ankles. I run my finger along her skin.

"You sure you don't want more company? Those girls were pretty hot."

I know she's teasing me. She has that wicked look in her eyes. "I just want you."

And fuck, it's true. Those girls might not have made the cut, but when have I ever sat in a club with just one woman?

Even when I'm dating someone, there are always others hanging around.

Maybe I do need another drink.

Melissa pulls her legs from my lap. "You brought me here to dance, right?"

"That I did."

I stand and take off my jacket, laying it across the seat. I hold out a hand for Melissa and help her up. Our booth is near the dance floor, so I lead her out beneath the flashing lights. The music blares, and well-dressed people dance around us.

My roommate at prep school taught me the secret to dancing with a woman. It isn't about the moves or even having great rhythm; it's all about making *her* look good.

Not that Melissa needs any help from me. There isn't a woman in the club as stunning as she is.

I put my hands on her hips and draw her in close, moving to the rhythm of the music. Her body moves with mine, and I run my hands up her back. She turns and tosses her hair over her shoulder, pressing her ass into my groin.

The bass reverberates through me, and my head is light. I let my thoughts go, focusing on the music, and Melissa's body moving with mine.

Parq isn't exclusive enough to avoid the occasional wannabe paparazzi, and I notice a guy snapping pictures of us from across the floor. I ignore him. It might mean some dumbass feature that makes the rounds on the internet for a few days, but fuck it. That shit is hard for a man like me to avoid. People are voyeurs. They like to think they're getting a peek into my world, especially when the pictures make them feel like they're looking in my windows without me knowing.

One song blends seamlessly into another. The DJ knows

his shit. People dance, and laugh, and cheer around us. Someone puts a hand on my arm, but she isn't Melissa, so I shrug her off and pivot away. We go to our booth, take more shots, and head back to the dance floor. Melissa laughs, and spins, and sings along to the lyrics. I keep my hands all over her, grabbing her ass, her hips, running my fingers through her hair. Nothing exists but the steady beat of the music and this woman who fills all of me.

I have no idea what time it is, and Melissa's body rubbing against me is driving me insane. Suddenly I have to get her out of this club. I need to take her back to the villa and fuck her until neither of us can breathe.

I dig my fingers into her ass and press my hard cock against her. "I need to get out of here. Now."

"Me, too."

We stagger out of the club and climb into the limo. I don't even wait until we start moving. I hike up her dress and push her panties to the side, thrusting my cock in her as soon as I have my pants undone. I'm wild with need for her. I pound her until we both come in a rush.

But I'm not finished. We stumble into the villa and don't make it past the entryway. I tear off my clothes and grab her, lifting her up with my hands on her ass. Her legs wrap around my waist and I hold her up against the wall. I fuck her madly, desperately. We stop before finishing. I'm too drunk to hold her up. I follow her down the hall to one of the bedrooms and bend her over the side of the bed. She calls my name, shouting her ecstasy while I thrust my cock in her—hard. An ache has lodged itself in my chest and I'm frantic to get rid of it.

I pull out and turn her over, pushing her up onto the bed with rough hands. I want to see her face when I come. I grab her ass and kiss her mouth. My cock pulses and I stiffen, the orgasm tearing through me. It seems to last forever, my dick throbbing as I empty myself into her.

I fall onto the bed, breathing hard. My head swims and my body is spent. The room seems to tilt and I close my eyes, laying my arm across my head. Melissa shifts next to me, but I have nothing left. I relax and fall into a numb sleep.

14

MELISSA

My eyes feel like they're lined with sandpaper. I open them slowly, waiting for the stabbing pain that the light will cause. I cringe, trying not to whimper. Yep, that hurts. My stomach is hollow and raw, and my mouth tastes sour. I need water. Lots of water. And ibuprofen. Lots of that, too.

Jackson is sprawled out on the bed, face down, his back moving slowly with his breathing. I roll off the bed, careful not to wake him. After the night we had, I'm sure he needs more time to sleep it off.

It seems odd that I have clothes on, although my dress is hiked up around my waist. My thong is wedged uncomfortably—even for a thong—in my ass crack. I'm pretty sure Jackson and I fucked each other until we passed out after getting back from the club. It must have been intense, because I'm sore between the legs.

I head for the bathroom and stop. It isn't there. I glance around the room. We aren't in the master, where we've slept all week. We must have stumbled into this bedroom last night. I put a hand to my aching head and walk to the other side of the room, shutting the bathroom door.

My hair is a disaster. "Sex hair" doesn't even begin to describe the mess atop my head. I don't have any of my things in this bathroom, so I smooth it down with my hands. I use the toilet and clean myself up as best I can with a wet washcloth.

What a night. I haven't partied that hard in years.

I tried to play hard-to-get when Jackson suggested buying more clothes, but the truth is, it sounded fun. And it was. I've never owned a sexier pair of shoes, and the dress made me feel amazing. Jackson's reaction didn't hurt, either.

I still can't fathom why he looks at me the way he does. No matter how good I feel all dressed up, I'm still just ... me. A small-town teacher with a fisherman for a daddy. Jackson has a parade of women: rich women, models, women who live the way he does. I feel like I've been looking in on his world from the outside, skirting along the edges with his hand on my back, guiding me along. But I can't come inside. Not really.

It was a rush to walk right up to the bouncer and get into the club. If looks could kill, those girls in line would have murdered me with their eyes, but it only made me laugh. People watch Jackson wherever we go, and nowhere was it more intense than at Parq.

He was completely in his element. Club staff at his beck and call, ready to do anything to make him happy. Women throwing themselves at him, oblivious to the fact that he was there with someone. Drinks flowing, music booming. He seemed a little distant, but we were pretty drunk.

And his claim that he could dance wasn't bullshit. He's almost as good on the dance floor as he is in bed—and that's saying something.

I rinse out my mouth with water and dry off my hands. Jackson is still asleep, so I let him be. I head upstairs to our room, grabbing a bottled water from the kitchen along the way. If Nathan or any of the staff are around, they're discreet enough to stay out of sight. I down some water, grab clean clothes, and head for the shower.

JACKSON BARELY SPEAKS OVER BREAKFAST. He looks at his phone, swiping his thumb over the screen. I drink my coffee, shifting uncomfortably in my seat. He hasn't said anything about leaving, but I notice one of the staff bringing our bags down and setting them by the front door. It feels odd that someone packed my things.

But none of it is really mine anyway.

Jackson avoids meeting my eyes, but still puts a gentle hand on my back as he leads me to the limo. I get in, and watch out the windows as we drive away. The clouds have parted and the sun is out; the water is sparkling. In no more than a minute, we leave the villa behind, the car gliding up the road toward the freeway.

Dread runs through me. I feel like I should say something, at least make small talk, but I can't think of anything to say. Jackson drinks a glass of whiskey in the limo and offers one to me. I turn him down. After last night, even the thought of alcohol makes me queasy.

He doesn't say much while we wait at the airport, just sips another drink in the executive lounge. Nor while we sit in our wide, first-class seats. He has a couple more whiskeys on the three-hour flight, and I start to wonder how he's going to drive me home after we land.

My breath catches in my throat when I realize—he won't

drive me home. We'll land in Seattle and he'll already have a car waiting to take me the three hours to Jetty Beach. This will be it. The end to our week.

And I'll probably never see him again.

I bite the inside of my cheek and stare out the window. I don't want to cry in front of him. I can sob my eyes out on the drive home, alone in some fucking limo—even though there's no reason for me to be upset. This is what I agreed to. One week, no strings. Wasn't I the one to say that first? No expectations, no worries about the future.

We both know we live in totally different worlds. He wanted to play with me for a while. Touch me and dress me up and fuck me with expensive shoes on. Tweet about his new mystery girl. I was a diversion, something for him to do to pass a few money-soaked days of his privileged life. He'll go back to his expensive-ass car, his condo in the city, his parties. His women. And I'll go back to my life. That's the deal, and it should be fine.

I can't understand why it hurts so much.

After we land, he leads me straight outside. I ask about baggage claim, but he says someone else will pick up our luggage. A limo waits at the curb, a driver in a crisp suit holding the door. I swallow hard. Is this it? Is this goodbye? Is he even going to say anything?

Jackson follows me into the limo, and I swipe the tears from my cheeks before he can see them. I can't look at him. I wish he would have let me go at the airport, instead of dragging out the agony. I know we're going to get his car, but I'm sure he'll send me off on my own after that.

Plus, I'm not sure he should drive.

"Hey," I say, gathering the nerve to speak. "Are you sure you should drive home right now?"

He looks up from his phone, his brow furrowed. “What?”

“I’m not trying to give you a hard time, but you’ve been drinking all day. Are you okay to drive?”

He glances around the limo, as if to make sure he knows where he is. “I’m not driving.”

“I know, but I figured we’re going to pick up your car, and then you’ll have to drive it home.”

“Oh, no. My car’s already been taken back to my place.” He gestures toward the opaque glass separating us from the driver. “He’ll take me home.”

I nod and settle back into the seat, tucking my legs under me. I glance out the window and see the freeway sign. We turn south. Jackson lives north. Is he going to drive all the way out to Jetty Beach with me?

The thought of three hours in the limo with him, while he stares at his phone, ignoring me, is worse than being sent off from the airport by myself. I turn away, biting my lip harder.

“Hey,” he says, his tone suddenly soft and gentle. “Are you okay?”

I nod, refusing to look at him.

“Fuck, Melissa, I’m sorry. Come here.”

Don’t do it, Melissa. He’s done with you. You’ll only make it worse.

His hands pull me to him and he wraps his arms around me. I lean into him, hearing the sound of his heartbeat. He kisses the top of my head and holds me tight. Tears burn my eyes, and my chest feels like it will burst.

After a while, I sit up and he lets his arms fall. We pass most of the drive in silence. That isn’t like Jackson. He doesn’t even look at his phone, just stares out the window, one hand resting on his chin. He doesn’t touch, or tease. He doesn't try to have me one last time for the road. He just sits, watching the scenery go by.

I must fall asleep, because I open my eyes and see the gateway sign to Jetty Beach. The car turns onto the main road through town and a fresh wave of nausea rolls through my stomach. A few minutes later, the car pulls up in front of my house.

I haven't thought much about what this moment will be like, how we'll say goodbye. A week ago, I would have thought it would be a passionate kiss on the doorstep. Maybe an offer of one last fuck to finish the week off right. I would let out a contented sigh, happy with the memories of an insane little adventure, and go back to living my life.

What I didn't count on was Jackson Bennett, staring at me with so much pain in his eyes.

He looks away, putting a hand over his mouth. The driver opens the door and Jackson casts one more glance at me, then gets out. I follow, shouldering my purse. He stops at my door and faces me, that same intense look in his blue eyes. I step up onto the porch, standing right in front of him.

He walks away.

Not a word. No awkward embrace of two people unsure of what to say. No kiss. No hands on my ass, nothing whispered in my ear. Just his hands in his pockets and his back to me as he walks down the path to the street. He gets back into the car, the driver closes the door, and just like that, he's gone.

15

JACKSON

By the time the driver pulls up to my building, I'm drunk as shit.

I started drinking again as soon as the limo pulled away from Melissa's house, and haven't really stopped on the three-hour drive to my place. I can't deal with this emptiness. It fucking sucks. I haven't felt this way since I was a kid. I don't *let* myself feel this way.

I'm Jackson motherfucking Bennett. I have so much money, I don't even know how much I'm worth; I pay other people to know. When I set out to do something, I do it. I'm driven, focused, and successful beyond even my wildest dreams.

But I still drove away from her.

Fuck. I'm so mad at myself, I can't think. The elevator opens and I stumbled inside. I manage to press the buttons and get out at the right place. My condo takes up the two top floors of an old restored building on Queen Anne. I own the whole thing, but one of my property management companies takes care of the other units. The lower floor is a wide-open living space, with a big kitchen that only caterers have ever used, a bar, and lots of seating. A balcony stretches along one entire side, with a pool, and an incredible view of the city skyline. I don't really live here; I use it for entertaining. My personal space is upstairs, and very few people ever see those rooms.

My phone controls everything in the house, including the locks. I swipe a button and the door to the stairway swishes open. I trudge up the stairs, and emerge into a wide living room. I have a huge TV mounted on the wall, a large sectional sofa, and art that someone else chose for me. Floor-to-ceiling windows flank a glass accordion door that takes up almost the entire wall. It leads to a balcony, but I only have a couple of lounge chairs. It's rare that I have people up here with me. As much as I hate being alone, I like my private space.

I toss my jacket on a chair and head for my bedroom. A few taps of my phone and the blinds close, and the flat screen facing my bed turns on. I flop down on the bed, my head still spinning.

"Bennett."

Dennis stands in my doorway, dressed as usual in an impeccable gray suit, his hair styled in a retro pompadour. Dennis is my Alfred, only younger and a hell of a lot gayer —and I don't have a Batcave. He lives in one of my condos downstairs, and is Tammi's counterpart. Where Tammi handles my business and travel needs, Dennis takes care of my condo, tends to my wardrobe, and knows how to throw an absolutely killer party, even on a moment's notice. I pay him a shit-ton of money to be available whenever I need him, and the arrangement suits us both.

Occasionally, some dumbass asks if it makes me uncomfortable to have a personal assistant with access to my house who is gay. It always makes me laugh. I'm man enough not to be threatened by a guy who might look at my ass. Besides, when Dennis tells me my ass looks good in Armani, I know I can trust his judgment.

I mumble something incoherent at him.

Dennis takes a step forward and sniffs. "Water, Tylenol, and probably dinner, yes? Or would you like to continue with ... what are you drinking today, Scotch?"

"Water." More Scotch is the last thing I need—it doesn't even sound good anymore. Dennis nods and leaves quietly.

My phone buzzes, and I glance at the screen. It's my father. I was wrong. A conversation with my father is the last thing I need.

Against my better judgment, I answer. "Dad."

"Jackson, have you heard from your mother lately?"

"I'm doing fine, how are you?" I ask, not bothering to disguise the sarcasm in my voice.

"Oh, for fuck's sake, Jack, answer the question."

I hate it when he calls me Jack. "She's in Costa Rica, taking surfing lessons."

Or fucking the surfing instructor. I really don't care. My parents are legally married, and my dad still bankrolls her life, but they haven't lived together for more than a few weeks at a time in years. They kept up appearances when I was a kid—although, looking back, I have no idea why. I had two nannies, and when I was old enough they sent me to boarding school. I was raised by teachers. It wouldn't have mattered, at least not to their kids, if they got a divorce. We weren't ever home with them anyway.

"Oh for the love of ... Costa Rica." He mumbles something else and hangs up. I shake my head and drop the phone on the bed again.

Dennis returns with an Asian chicken salad, a tall glass

of ice water, four Tylenol, an Airborne tablet fizzing in another glass, and an artisan roll, already buttered.

I sit up on the edge of the bed. "Do I pay you enough?"

"Yes." Dennis cracks a smile. "Yes, you do."

"Good."

"Company tonight?" Dennis asks. "It's late, but it *is* Saturday. I could put the word out, do a spontaneous after-party."

"No," I say, shaking my head. "I don't want a single fucking person here."

"Fair enough. Anything else?"

"No, I'm fine. I need to sleep this off. Go ... do whatever it is you do when you're not here."

"Text me if you need something," Dennis says as he walks out of the room.

I down half the water, and eat some of the salad. But I still feel like crap.

What the fuck is happening to me?

When I thought up this plan, sitting on Melissa's couch, I felt like a kid with a new toy. I was going to take her out, show her a great time, blow her mind.

And then she went and blew mine.

I was paralyzed on the drive from the airport to Jetty Beach. The closer we got to the coast, the bigger the gaping hole in my chest grew. By the time we turned into the little town, the feeling was unbearable. I stared out the window, convinced we were going to get in an accident and she'd be killed. I imagined a tsunami crashing in, taking out the whole town, and Melissa with it. What if something bad happened to her, and I wasn't around? I was about to drop her right back into her life, and leave her there.

Why couldn't I deal with that? Why do I feel like I'm dying inside?

I've never been with a woman I couldn't just walk away from. Usually I get bored, or they get too needy, and I cut things off. Simple. I tried a real relationship for a while, tried staying committed to her, even when the fun wore off. But in the end, I didn't see the point. We mostly just made each other miserable, so I ended it and moved on. I walked away.

Walking away from Melissa wasn't the same.

I couldn't bring myself to say goodbye. The word had been too much, I couldn't utter it. So I turned around and left without saying anything. I got in the limo, and poured myself a drink. It wasn't my finest moment.

But, fuck, I'm confused. I don't understand all these goddamn feelings, because I've never felt any of them before. I don't even know what they are.

I leave the rest of my dinner uneaten, and crash back on my bed. My phone blinks with notifications, but I don't care. I type out a tweet, a voice in the back of my head telling me I might regret it in the morning, and toss my phone onto the nightstand.

I leave the TV on so I won't have to deal with the silence, and go to sleep.

16

MELISSA

I allow myself one evening to melt into a puddle of despair. I cry. I eat ice cream, then I wish I didn't eat the ice cream because my stomach is still sour from last night's alcohol. I go to bed, wrap myself in a blanket, and sleep it off.

I get up the next morning, ready to let the bootstrap-pulling commence. John Simon did not raise a girl who will let her life fall apart over some guy. I will let the week be what it was: a wild experience I'll later look back on with fondness. *Wow, remember that time I ran off with that rich guy for a week? That was so insane...*

It was insane. And wonderful.

And utterly terrifying.

Which is probably why Jackson's text makes me want to puke.

My phone dings and I'm afraid to look. I tell myself it must be Nicole, checking to see if I'm home. I pick it up and swipe my finger across the screen. It's Jackson.

Didn't leave things very well. Sorry about that.

I blow out a breath and send a reply. I'm hurt and angry,

and I'm not going to let him get away with it. *Nope. You didn't.*

My phone dings again. *I'm not sure what to do now.*

I stare out the window, my phone dangling from my hand. Is this Jackson, or did someone else get hold of his phone? Jackson always knows what to do. He takes what he wants, when he wants it.

Is he trying to fix this? Is there even anything to fix?

Me neither. I hit send, and wait. He doesn't reply.

A few hours later, my phone rings. I gasp, a jolt of adrenaline surging through me. I breathe out a sigh of relief—or is it sadness?—when I see Nicole's name on the screen.

"Hey, Nicole."

"Mel! Are you back?"

"Yeah, I'm home."

"Okay, don't tell me anything yet. I want to hear all about your week, but in person."

"Sure."

"Wait, are you all right? What's wrong?"

"I don't really want to talk about it yet."

I hear Nicole take a deep breath. "All right, I won't ask. Listen, the weather's really beautiful so we're having a bonfire on the beach tonight. Just a few people, it's no big deal. I know you just got home, but I thought you still might want to come."

Anything sounds better than sitting at home alone. "Yeah, that sounds great."

"Yeah? Good. I miss you. We're here, so come up anytime."

"Sounds good, Nic. Thanks."

Later that evening, I drive up to Ryan and Nicole's place. Ryan restored an old church that sits on a bluff overlooking the ocean. The main part of the building is his photography studio, and they live in an apartment off to the side. I can see

Nicole's touches already melding with Ryan's bachelor pad. It actually looks really nice. She hasn't girlied it up too much, just added a few things to make it look like theirs. It's sweet.

Ryan and his brothers already sit around a fledgling fire. Cody is the spitting image of Ryan, only slightly taller and slightly less intense. Hunter isn't related, but he grew up in the Jacobsen house. The three act like brothers, anyway. They joke and insult each other continuously.

Nicole and I sit in camping chairs, facing the fire, with the ocean beyond. The waves beat their steady rhythm against the sand, and the light fades as the sun goes down.

Cody's girlfriend Jennifer stands away from the fire, waving her hand in front of her face as if the tiny drift of smoke offends her. Five minutes later, she announces she can't stay, and walks back up the beach to the house.

Cody watches her go, but doesn't make any move to go after her.

"That was ... awkward," Hunter says. He pokes a stick in the flames and moves the wood around.

"Quit messing with it," Ryan says, smacking Hunter's stick away with his own.

Nicole gives me a look and shrugs her shoulders. I don't know Jennifer well, but she has a superior air that bothers me. Cody seems relieved that she's gone, but he doesn't say anything about it.

Ryan grabs a beer from the cooler and holds it out to me.

"Thanks, but I'm sticking with water. I think I need to do a cleanse or something to flush out all the booze."

"Sounds like you had a good time," Ryan says.

I stuff my hands in the pockets of my hoodie. At least I'm back in my own clothes. "Yeah."

"I can't take it anymore," Nicole says. "You've said like,

two things since you got here."

I can't see Nicole's face, but Ryan gives her a confused look. She kicks sand in his direction.

"Right, yeah," Ryan says, standing. "Hey, will you guys help me get the food? And more beer?"

Hunter looks at Ryan like he's nuts, but Cody gets the hint. "Yeah, sure, man." He turns to Hunter. "Let's go."

Ryan leans down and kisses Nicole, then the three guys walk back toward the house.

Nicole turns in her seat to face me. "Talk to me."

I take a deep breath. I don't even know where to begin. "It was ... I don't know Nicole. It was so much."

"It looked like you guys were having fun the whole time."

"How would you even know that? Oh, right. You followed the whole fucking week on Twitter."

"I'm sorry," she says. "That was shitty of me, wasn't it? I was just so worried about you. And you only texted me maybe twice the entire time you were gone."

"Yeah, I kind of ignored my phone a lot."

"So, was it good or wasn't it? I'm confused."

So am I. "It was good, I guess. No—I don't *guess*. It was fucking incredible. He was incredible. He was nothing like I thought he'd be. When he showed up at my house and said he wanted to take me away, I figured sure, this guy is hot, and I want to fuck his brains out, so why not? This will be fun. No big deal, just casual, then we go back to our lives. I'm single, I can get away with this."

"But...?"

"But he wasn't just a hot, cocky as shit, rich guy. He was those things, but you should have seen him when we were alone. There's this side of him that is so affectionate and sweet. He stared at me all the time and never stopped touching me. And it wasn't like he only did it for an audience. I mean, yeah, he paraded me around a little bit, but most of the time, we just hung out, the two of us. We stayed in this ridiculous mansion on the beach, and watched movies, and ate a lot, and drank too much. We laid out in the sun by the pool, and laughed and joked, and made fun of each other. Like normal people, you know?"

"Was he not supposed to be normal?"

"No," I say, my voice emphatic. "No, because he isn't normal. Everywhere we went, people were like, 'Yes, Mr. Bennett, right this way, Mr. Bennett, very good, Mr. Bennett.' People stare at him and fall all over themselves to make sure he has whatever he wants."

"Is that the problem, then? His life is too different?"

"That's on the list." I pause for a moment, and when I speak again my voice is quiet. "The problem is, I wasn't supposed to care when this was over."

Nicole grabs my hand and squeezes. "Well, what happens now? When are you going to see him again?"

"I don't know. He left without saying goodbye when he dropped me off, so I figured, that's it. He's done and it's over. I was kind of okay with that this morning. At least I knew where things stood. But then he texted me."

"But that's good, right?"

"I guess." I lean my head back. "I'm so confused."

"Maybe this isn't the best time to bring this up, but have you seen the article yet?"

"What article?"

She purses her lips. "I guess that means no."

"What is it?" I ask, not sure I wanted to know.

"It's totally not a big deal. Just some pictures of you guys in a club together, mostly. Do you want to see, or just leave it?"

I hold out my hand. "No, I'll look."

She taps her phone's screen a few times and hands it to me. There's a picture of me and Jackson, dancing at the club. We're facing each other, his hand low on my back, pressing me against him. My face is turned up to his, my hair falling in waves behind me. We're both smiling, our eyes locked on each other.

I read the caption at the bottom. *Jackson Bennett, one of the hottest (and wealthiest!) bachelors in the country, dances with an unknown woman at Parq in San Diego. Could this finally be a glimpse of his infamous Sassy Girl? Bennett's large Twitter following has been in an uproar over his mysterious tweets, to the point that #whoissassygirl has been trending on the social media platform.*

"Son of a bitch." I hand the phone back to Nicole.

"Well, you look unbelievable in this picture, so at least there's that. Where did you get those shoes?"

"Fuck the shoes. That, right there, is the problem. He lives like that: parties and clubs and pictures of him going around the internet. I have no idea how to handle that."

"Yeah, it's pretty intense. I thought the Twitter stuff was crazy enough."

"I haven't even looked."

"Really? Yikes."

"What do you mean, yikes?" I ask, sitting up to look at her.

"No, it's not bad. Well, some of it is. But mostly it's fine. People are intrigued by you. The bad stuff isn't a big deal. People think they can get away with saying anything online. It's best to just ignore them."

I pull up Twitter on my phone, knowing it's probably a bad idea. I go to Jackson's profile and scroll through his tweets. There are a lot of pictures of me, but none of them quite show my face. He tweeted my shoes at the club; a picture of me from behind, standing on the beach; a close up, my face turned just enough so you can't quite see me. His feed is filled with them.

One shows me curled up on the couch, a drink perched on my knee. You can actually see my face, although I'm looking away. I read his tweet.

This girl. This girl right here.

My breath catches and I swallow the lump that suddenly appears in my throat.

I click through some of the comments. Most of them are questions about who I am, or where we are, or what I'm wearing. One picture is a close up of my mouth and some jackass replied with a comment about me having a mouth good for dick sucking. A lot of replies tear him a new one, but it's still disconcerting to see.

"This is what I'm talking about," I say. "Who lives like this?"

"Ryan says he takes really great pictures, especially considering he just uses his phone. The composition on these is really good."

I look sideways at her. "Seriously?"

"Well, they are. Did you see his tweet from last night?"

I scroll up.

Empty condo. Empty life. My chest is hollow. There isn't enough Scotch in the world.

He hasn't tweeted anything since.

"He was probably drunk off his ass last night. He drank all the way here, and probably kept going the whole way back to his place."

"Well, why do you think he would do that?"

"Don't use your know-it-all voice on me, Mrs. Jacobsen."

Nicole puts a hand to her chest and laughs. "Oh my god,

it freaks me out when you call me that. But really, don't you think he's sad because you aren't with him?"

I think about his texts from earlier. "Maybe."

"Maybe, my ass."

"And a hot ass it is," Ryan says, appearing from behind us with a tray full of food.

"You should at least text him. Tell him you're thinking about him."

"I don't know if that's a good idea. I should let this end before it gets worse."

"But what if it gets better?"

I take a deep breath and stare at my phone. Nicole kind of has a point, and Jackson did reach out to me. He straight up said he was sorry, and I wasn't exactly receptive.

And the truth is, I miss him. Terribly. That realization scares the shit out of me, but denying it isn't going to do me any good.

I open text messaging and type.

Sorry I didn't say much earlier. I'm confused. I know we said a week and that would be all. Am I the only one who thinks a week isn't enough? You said you wouldn't fuck with me, so don't. Is this over?

I watch the fire crackle, half-listening to the conversations around me, waiting. Nicole stands up and Ryan wraps his arms around her. Cody cracks a joke about them getting a room.

After long moments, my phone dings with Jackson's reply. *It isn't over for me. I miss the fuck out of you.*

I laugh, tears springing to my eyes. Nicole glances over at me and smiles.

I'm still not sure what this means, and the implications scare the crap out of me. But I know I can't let him go so easily.

17

JACKSON

"Jackson."

I blink, realizing Tammi asked me a question. I have no idea what she just said.

"Sorry. Distracted." I've been thinking about Melissa. I dropped her off at her place five days ago and I haven't been able to get her out of my head. Aside from a few brief texts, I haven't spoken to her, let alone seen her. I've been too busy catching up after my impromptu week off. But she's always there, lingering in the corners of my consciousness.

"I can see that. I need a signature." She sits across the desk from me, dressed in a perfectly tailored pencil skirt and light blue blouse, her red hair pulled up. She adjusts her glasses and shuffles through a small stack of paperwork she brought in, her wedding ring catching the light.

Tammi is officially my longest-running female relationship, and I have a feeling it's because she's been happily married since before I hired her. She's attractive in a businesslike way, and once in a while I wonder what she looks like with her glasses off and hair down. But she's never been available to me, so I don't really think of her that way. Which is probably just as well. Tammi is indispensable, and if I'd ever slept with her she'd be long gone by now.

I glance at the contract, initial where she stuck Post-it notes, and sign on the last page. I already reviewed it, twice, so my signature is just a final formality.

"What do I have on my calendar this afternoon?" I ask.

She glances at her phone. "You have a four o'clock with the people from Tech Solutions."

Damn. I can't cancel that one. "What about tomorrow?"

"Nothing that can't be moved."

"Good." I want to drive out to see Melissa as soon as I can, but it looks like I'll have to wait until morning.

"You have a banquet on Saturday night, and you need to be in the office Wednesday. Other than that, it's mostly conference calls and things I can reschedule if you need. Where are you off to this time? Or will you decide at the airport?"

I can hear the amusement in her voice. Tammi generally disapproves of my personal life, but she rarely comments on it.

"No flights."

"Nice deflection."

"I'm not deflecting."

She arches an eyebrow at me and looks at her phone, swiping her thumb across the screen. "I'll email you the rest of the documentation by end of business tomorrow."

"Good."

I expect her to get up and go back to her office. We're finished. But she lingers, pressing her lips together.

"Is there something else?" I ask.

"I'm just wondering what this is all about."

I lean back in my chair, pitching my fingertips together. I know what she means. Tammi can talk to me in ways that would get anyone else fired, but I'm not sure I want her asking me about Melissa. "What *this* are you referring to?"

"The woman in Jetty Beach."

"What about her?" I ask, not bothering to disguise the defensiveness in my voice.

She pauses, as if choosing her words before answering. "Nothing about *her*, specifically. But I've worked for you for almost a decade and I've never seen you like this."

It bothers me that Tammi can see something I'm trying to keep to myself. I flaunted my fling with Melissa, enjoying the attention online. That part is public. But I know that isn't what Tammi is talking about. There's something else happening, and even I'm not sure what it is. Until I know, I'm not prepared to discuss it with anyone—particularly my assistant.

"It's not a big deal. I'm just having some fun with her."

"Hmm," she says.

"You disapprove?" Not that it's any of her business.

She shrugs. "I didn't say that. You're a grown up, you can do what you want. Besides, it could be worse. My friend in New York works for a guy who makes the women he sleeps with sign a contract."

I raise an eyebrow. I'm familiar with the practice. "I don't need a contract."

"No, I suppose you don't." She stands and gathers up the paperwork. "I'll send your four o'clock to the conference room."

My meeting runs long, turning into dinner and drinks at Canlis. Their seafood is good, but I'm not in the mood. I nurse my drink and make a graceful exit as soon as I can.

Home isn't much better. Too quiet. Dennis could take care of that if I ask. Even on a Thursday night, he could have my condo bursting with people in an hour. Music. Drinks. It's warm—women would strip down and jump in the pool. I haven't done any of my usual socializing in weeks. Not since I met Melissa.

That's a disturbing thought.

I strip down to a t-shirt and underwear, and pour myself a glass of Scotch. My condo is too quiet, so I turn on a mindless action flick and sit on the couch with my drink.

I glance at my phone, thinking I should text her. Or call. It's after eleven, but she'll probably be up. I take a sip of the Scotch. It's good, but it will never taste as good as it did off Melissa's skin.

I don't want to text her. Even hearing her voice won't be enough. I want her. I want to smell her, feel her. Touch her.

What the fuck am I waiting for?

She's three hours away, and I have no desire to drive all that way in the middle of the night. But what good is all my money if I don't use it? I call my driver and tell him to drink a Red Bull and pick me up in ten minutes.

I DOZE for most of the drive. The back of my limo is comfortable as hell, and the sound of the tires on the road lulls me into a light sleep. I wake when the car pulls to a stop and the engine turns off.

I glance at the time. Two thirty-seven. I haven't told Melissa I'm coming.

I get out of the car and tell my driver to wait until I'm inside, then go find a hotel. I rub my eyes, trying to wake up, and walk up to her door. Her house is dark, the street quiet. Her garage is closed, but I'm sure she's home. I lift my hand to knock, and it occurs to me she might not answer the door in the middle of the night. I want to surprise her, not scare her.

I send her a quick text. *Melissa. Wake up.*

I lean against the door, waiting for her reply. I'm just about to text again, when her message comes through. *What's wrong? Are you okay?*

I'm outside.

There's a pause and a light flicks on, filtering through the curtain.

Outside here?

Yes. I knock.

I hear footsteps. She opens the door a crack and peeks out. Her hair is disheveled, and she's wearing nothing but a striped t-shirt and panties.

My cock jumps to attention and my tiredness instantly disappears. Melissa stares at me for a moment, her mouth open. I want to devour those lips, but she looks so dazed.

She backs up and I follow her inside, closing the door behind me. Her whole house smells like her. I stand there for a moment, just breathing it in, like an addict getting his hands on his drug of choice. I've been lifeless since I left her on her doorstep. Just being near her makes me feel alive again.

"Hi." She rubs her eyes and tries to smooth down her hair.

I take a step closer. "Hi. I thought I'd surprise you."

"You're good at that."

Her nipples are hard beneath her tight shirt. I love the way she looks, all tousled and sleepy.

"Is it a good surprise?" I ask, moving closer still.

"Yeah," she says, her voice breathy.

It's all the encouragement I need.

I slip my hands around her waist and pull her against me. Her body is smooth and warm, so familiar. I bury my face in her neck and breathe her in while she threads her arms around me.

"I missed you," I whisper into her ear. I trail kisses down her neck, tasting her skin. God, she feels so good.

Melissa pulls back and finds my mouth with hers. She parts her lips and I slide my tongue in. I grab her ass, digging my fingers into her taut flesh. I want every inch of her. My cock is so hard I can hardly stand it, and I groan as I press it against her body.

I run my hand beneath her shirt and hold her breast. She rubs against my cock. I kiss her, hard, the feel of her mouth sending me into a frenzy.

"Jackson, I need you inside me. Now."

We stumble toward her bedroom, pulling off our clothes. I lay her down on the bed and climb on top of her, settling between her legs. Her pussy is slick and hot, ready for me. I kiss her again and thrust myself inside.

It's unreal. She feels so fucking good, I could come in her right now. She's hot, and soft, and tight. I love being inside her.

Melissa moans as my cock goes in and out. I kiss her mouth, her neck, her breasts. I run my tongue over the hard nub of her nipple and she arches her back.

"You feel so good." I dig my cock into her, feeling the tip bottom out. She leans her head back and calls out. I hold there, feeling the sweet, hot folds of her pussy surrounding me.

Something changes. She covers her eyes with a hand

and her body trembles. I ease up on the pressure and gently shift her hand away from her face. Tears glisten in her eyes.

"Baby, what's wrong?"

Her voice is so soft. "You left."

Damn it. I lean my forehead down to hers, our noses brushing against each other. "I shouldn't have."

"I didn't think I'd see you again. I thought—"

"Shh." I put a finger to her lips. "I'm here now."

"Then fuck me harder. I need to know you're real."

I pull out and plunge in again. Her fingers dig into my back, her eyes locked with mine.

"You want it harder?"

"Yes," she says between thrusts. "God, yes."

I pull out and flip her over, guiding her hips so she's on her knees. She holds onto the headboard, arching her back. I grab her delicious ass and plunge into her pussy from behind. I reach around with one hand, teasing her clit with my fingers. She grinds her hips into my groin, moaning with each thrust.

"Jackson, I'm gonna come." She tosses her hair over one shoulder and looks back at me. Her lids are half closed, her cheeks flushed. Fuck, she's so sexy.

I pound her harder, feeling my orgasm build. "That's right, baby. Come for me."

"Oh god, Jackson," she says, her voice tinged with urgency.

Her pussy contracts, clenching around my dick. It's more than I can take. I explode inside her, waves of intensity rolling through me. I hold her hips, pushing my cock in deep as I empty into her.

We pause for a moment, catching our breath. She slides off of me and settles down onto the bed. I lay next to her, drawing her close in my arms. Her quick breathing matches mine. I can still feel the pulses of pleasure reverberating through me, the feel of her body enveloping me. No woman has ever felt so good. I fit inside her like she's made just for me. I kiss her forehead and let her scent fill me. My body is spent, my eyes so heavy I can feel myself drifting off to sleep already. But I've never felt so whole.

18

JACKSON

"Jackson, wake up."

The urgency in Melissa's voice wakes me with a start. I'm confused for a moment as to where I am. This isn't San Diego. Or my condo.

Right, Melissa's house.

I stretch my arms over my head. "What time is it?"

"Seven-thirty."

I groan and roll to my side. "Why are we awake?"

"Come on, Jackson, get up."

I turn onto my back and force my eyes open. She has sage-green walls, a distressed white dresser, and a mirror with a brushed nickel frame. "This room looks like Dennis designed it."

"Am I supposed to know Dennis?" she asks. She sits next to me, holding the sheet over her breasts. Tangled dark hair falls around her face.

"He's my assistant."

"I thought Tammi was your assistant."

I prop myself up, my elbow resting on the bed. "I have two."

She shakes her head slowly. “Of course you have two assistants. Damn it, stop distracting me.”

I trace the line of her collarbone. My dick stirs beneath the sheets. Maybe waking up early isn’t such a bad idea. “I love to distract you.”

“Oh no, not right now.” She swats my hand away. “You have to get dressed and get the fuck out of here.”

My mouth drops open. I literally have no idea what to say to that.

Melissa is already off the bed, pulling on clothes. “Seriously, Jackson, we don’t have much time.”

I narrow my eyes, a sharp spike of anger running through me. I came all this way, in the middle of the night. Is she kicking me out? “What the fuck, Melissa?”

She yanks her t-shirt down. “My dad is going to be here in, like, ten minutes. At the most.”

An odd sensation worms its way through me. I freeze. “Your dad?”

“Yes, my dad. So get up and put some clothes on. All of your clothes. It would really be better if you’re gone before he gets here.”

I stare at her. She wants to get me out of the house before her dad comes over? Are we fucking teenagers, afraid to get caught by our parents? “You’re kidding, right?”

“No, I’m not. Get dressed.”

The thought of meeting her father should send me running for the door, but fuck if I’m going to let her chase me off like some kid. The initial jolt of fear is replaced by stubborn resolve. “I’ll get dressed, but I’m not going anywhere.”

Melissa lets out a breath and puts a hand to her forehead. “Listen, my dad’s old school. He knows I’m a grown woman—he isn’t stupid—but seeing a man in my house first thing in the morning will give him a heart attack. So let's not put my dad in the hospital today, m'kay?"

I stand and slide on my underwear. "How long will he be here?"

"Not long—probably just a few minutes, really. He's heading out on the boat today and he needs to stop by before he goes. It's just a thing he does."

I pull on my pants. "How about I take you both to breakfast, then?"

"He won't have time. He's going out to drop the first crab pots of the season. It's a little early for it, but he says the ocean is speaking to him or some shit, and he knows where the crab will be. Which means he has to come here first."

"I... what?"

"Fishermen are literally the most superstitious people on the planet. He has to see me before he goes out to drop the first pots, or the crab will all go extinct or something."

I stare at her again. I have no idea what she's talking about. "So, you're kicking me out because your dad will be shocked to see a man here?"

"Yes, exactly."

"That's fucked up."

She stops, her hand on the doorknob. "Jackson, I haven't told my dad about you."

I'm livid. Why the hell does that piss me off so much? "Why?"

She whirls around. "What should I say to him? 'I met this rich, cocky motherfucker in a bar and he took me to California and fucked my brains out for a week?' Believe me, you do not want me to tell my dad that story."

I don't understand what's happening. Why do I care whether or not she tells her father about me? I certainly haven't told *my* father about *her*. Of course, my father is an asshole and I avoid talking to him at all costs. But Melissa and her dad have an actual relationship. Why is she hiding this?

Is there a *this*?

Fuck.

"Come on, Melissa." I follower her out to her living room, buttoning my shirt. "You said yourself, he knows you're a grown woman."

She pulls her hair up and ties it into a messy bun as she walks. "You don't understand about my dad. I'm his baby girl. He's really a big teddy bear, but when it comes to me, he can be pretty fierce."

"And you don't think I can handle fierce?" I say, my voice sharp.

"No, I'm sure you can, especially if fierce is in a suit and tie. Look, you live in a world where everyone respects you, or wants to kiss your ass—or both. My dad won't be impressed by your money. He's not going to have any idea who Jackson Bennett is. And, fuck, look at you."

I finish tucking in my shirt and look down at myself. "What?"

"You're ... god, Jackson, you're gorgeous. But you look like a fucking model. I don't know how to explain you to him."

The rumble of an engine comes from outside. Melissa's face pales.

I smirk. "That him?"

She nods, her eyes wide.

"Looks like I get to meet daddy."

I cuff the sleeves of my shirt while Melissa answers the door. Her father is a burly man with a thick chest, his dark hair and beard peppered with gray. He and Melissa have the same dark brown eyes, although his are creased at the edges. His face looks weathered, full of deep lines across his tanned skin. His beige t-shirt says *Carhartt* across the front, and his faded jeans hang over a pair of brown boots.

"Morning, princess," he says, leaning in to kiss Melissa's cheek.

He hasn't noticed me yet. I stand near the door to her kitchen, an odd sensation in my gut. I'm not afraid, exactly. I'm nervous in a way I can't remember feeling since I was a kid, but it isn't fear.

His eyes find me and he stops, his smile instantly gone.

"Daddy," she says, "this is my friend Jackson Bennett. Jackson, this is my father, John Simon."

I step forward and hold out my hand. "Pleasure to meet you, Mr. Simon."

John takes my hand. His skin is rough and calloused, his grip firm. He squeezes a little harder. "Jackson."

I keep my expression carefully neutral. His instant dislike for me is clear on his face. I can see something of what Melissa was trying to tell me. This man will not be easy to win over.

But I'm great with people.

I open my mouth to ask him a question, but he cuts me off before I can speak.

"Are you dating my daughter?"

Melissa puts a hand to her forehead. "Daddy."

"It's a fair question," John says, never taking his eyes off me.

I give him a careful smile. "Melissa is an amazing woman, and I've been fortunate enough to spend some time with her recently."

"Huh," John says. His eyes swing to Melissa. "When were you going to tell me about your boyfriend?"

Boyfriend? God, that word. I hate that word. I am not a

fucking boy. However, it's nice to watch John direct his scrutiny at Melissa instead of me. She puts her hands on her hips.

"Daddy, Jackson isn't exactly..." She pauses, her eyes flicking toward me. "What I mean is..."

"Melissa isn't sure whether she's going to keep me around."

"Huh," John says again. His sharp eyes move up and down, taking me in. He's sizing me up, but I can't read his face. "All right, then. Nice to meet you, Jackson."

Melissa gapes at her father. I put my hands in my pockets and wait while John brings out a worn, wooden keychain shaped like a crab.

"For luck," John says, holding it out to Melissa. She takes it and squeezes, then hands it back to him. He kisses her on the cheek again. "Thanks, princess."

"Of course, Daddy. Be safe out there, okay?"

"Always. You know me. There's old fishermen, and there's bold fishermen. I'm aiming for old."

Melissa smiles and hugs her father.

John tips his head to me. "See you treat this woman right. There's none like her."

"You have my word."

John leaves, and Melissa closes the door behind him. She leans against the door and breathes out a long breath.

"All that drama for what, a two-minute visit?" I'm irritated with her, but oddly proud of the way John Simon looked at me. I start unbuttoning my shirt as I walk back to her bedroom. "I'm going back to bed."

"I'm not sure who that was, but there's no way it was my dad," she says as she follows me.

I let my shirt drop to the floor and pull off my pants.

"What did you think he was going to do? Threaten to hurt me?"

"Maybe. It wouldn't be the first time. He's universally hated every man I've ever dated."

"He didn't think much of me." I lay down and pull up the covers.

She sits on the edge of the bed. "Are you kidding? He actually liked you."

I raise an eyebrow. "Why are you so shocked?"

"Because this is a first," she says, looking away. She clears her throat. "I don't think I can sleep. I'm going to go shower."

I grab her hand before she can get away, and gently pull. I'm too sleepy, and she smells too good, to stay mad. "Bring that hot ass over here."

She climbs into bed and tucks herself against me. My cock swells as her ass presses against it, but more than anything, I just want to feel her. I hug her close, my hand on her belly, my face in her hair.

At first, she feels stiff, like she doesn't want to be here. I'm about to relent and tell her to just get up, when she relaxes into me. She takes a deep breath and nestles in, arching her back a little.

"How long can you stay?" she asks.

"I'm supposed to go to a banquet tomorrow."

"What sort of banquet?"

"Some kind of benefit. I can't remember what it's for. I pay Tammi to remember those things." I run my hand up her ribcage to the bottom of her breast. My eyes are heavy, but she's so sweet and warm. "Do you want to come with me?"

She's quiet for a moment and I almost drift off. "Do you want me to come?"

"That's why I asked."

She pauses again. "Sure, I'd love to."

I slide my hand back down to her belly, feeling a strange sense of satisfaction. I can't remember the last time I cared about winning someone's approval, but I like being the one man Melissa's father didn't hate on sight. Despite what I said to her, I knew. I saw it in his face. He was skeptical, and cautious—and I respect the hell out of him for it—but despite that, he looked at me with acceptance.

That probably should scare the fuck out of me, but somehow it doesn't.

19

MELISSA

Jackson's surprise visit leaves me reeling.

Despite being half asleep and more than a little bewildered, I wanted to cry with relief when he showed up at my door. I've barely spoken to him since he left last week, and although he texted at least once a day, saying he missed me several times, I didn't know when I'd see him again. I was afraid to ask. I wasn't sure what I wanted the answer to be.

I spent a week with this man, and regardless of how incredible of a week it was, I'm freaked out by how attached I feel—how intensely I missed him. I've never felt this way about anyone before, and it isn't just that I missed how he can fuck me into a coma. I missed the way he touched me, the way he looked at me. The way his eyes narrow when he smiles. I missed his smell, and the feel of his warm body next to mine at night. My own bed felt so cold.

Seeing him again is wonderful, but it also scares the fuck out of me.

My dad didn't help. I feel so bad for trying to make Jackson leave before my dad could see him, but I expected it to get ugly. My dad is usually somewhere between aloof and openly hostile when he meets a man I'm dating. I know Jackson can handle anything my dad can dish out—that wasn't my worry. But depending on how far my dad decided to push, Jackson could have decided I'm not worth the hassle of a contentious father. I thought my dad would drive him away, and I wasn't sure I could handle that.

Dad's response to Jackson completely caught me off guard. He said *Nice to meet you*. He's literally never acted that way toward a man I'm dating. Instead of filling me with relief, the fact that my dad was friendly only scared me more. Are Jackson and I dating? Is this turning into a relationship? I still don't know what this is, and my dad seemed ready to welcome him into the fucking family.

Either that, or Dad could already tell it was nothing. Maybe he sensed Jackson wasn't here to stay, so he wasn't worth getting upset over.

That thought doesn't make me feel better.

I spend Friday showing Jackson around town—not that there's a lot to show, but I have fun taking him to some of my favorite places. We eat fish and chips for lunch (and I manage to pay without my damn card being declined), stop by the art gallery he's buying, and drive past the school where I work.

His driver brought him to town, but I don't think we need to drive around in a limo so we rumble around in my old Ford pickup. He laughs at my truck, but I love that old thing. It isn't much to look at, but it's sturdy as fuck. Jackson seems to appreciate it more when I tell him I was in an accident a few years ago and the other car was definitely on the losing end of that interaction.

We stay at my house again that night. I'm glad my only neighbors are elderly and neither of them can hear very well—otherwise they would get an earful. Jackson and I make up for lost time, fucking on the couch, up against the wall, on the kitchen table, and in the shower. We fall into bed that night, utterly exhausted.

Saturday morning, Jackson calls for his driver to pick us up early. He says we need time to get to the banquet. I doze for the first part of the drive, still tired from the night before. Jackson spends most of the trip on the phone, talking business. I love seeing that side of him; his cold, calculating voice is such a turn-on. By the time the driver pulls up in front of his building, I'm ready to rip my panties off and jump in his lap.

He leads me into a gorgeous, old brick building. It's been beautifully restored, with lavish furnishings and a sparkling crystal chandelier in the lobby. We get into an elevator that takes us to the top floor.

I try not to gape like a small-town hick when we walk into his condo. Everything is sleek and modern—masculine, but not just an expanse of dull gray. He has a big sectional sofa facing a huge wall-mounted TV, a gorgeous kitchen with bar stools pulled up to the island, and an entire wall of glass. I wander over to the floor-to-ceiling windows. It looks like every iconic picture of the Seattle skyline was taken from this spot.

Jackson stands behind me and slides his hands around my waist.

"This view is insane," I say.

"It's why I bought the building. I'm glad you like it."

"Bennett."

We both turn at the voice behind us. A slim man in a well-tailored suit stands in the living room. His dark hair is styled in a tall swoop and he wears black-rimmed glasses.

"Dennis, this is Melissa," Jackson says.

Dennis steps forward and takes my hand, bringing it up to his lips. "Melissa, it's an absolute pleasure."

I feel my face flush. "Thank you, Dennis. It's nice to meet you too."

Dennis shares a glance with Jackson, his eyebrows raised. Does he look surprised?

"We have a black tie benefit tonight," Jackson says. "Melissa needs something to wear, and we have to leave in an hour."

Dennis looks me up and down, a grin stealing over his face. "Finally, you give me something fun to do. Look at you. I wish you'd given me more of a heads up, Bennett, but at least I have something here to work with."

I want to wilt under his scrutiny. He isn't the least bit shy, pulling my hair back and running his hands down my shoulders and arms. Jackson doesn't seem to think there's anything unusual about his assistant practically fondling me. His phone rings, and he walks a short distance away to answer it.

"Your coloring is amazing," Dennis says. He takes a few pictures of me with his phone. "I'll bring a few choices, but I think I already know exactly what to put you in."

Dennis leaves. Jackson finishes his phone call and wanders into the kitchen. "Hungry? There's probably something in here."

"I'm fine. Does Dennis always show up like that when you come home?"

"He gets an alert," he says, like it's the most normal thing in the world.

"Of course he does. Did you ever figure out what this event is for?"

His phone rings again and he smiles. "Perfect timing. I'll find out." He answers. "Hey Tammi. Yes, I'm home. Okay.

No, that's fine, they can wait until next week. I'll tell them to fuck off. It isn't my fault they ran their company into the ground. Look, there's a reason they're selling, and it isn't because they're the geniuses they think they are. All right, just keep me posted. What am I attending tonight? That was generous of me. No, I have a date." He winks at me. "Are we all set for transportation? Perfect. See you Monday."

He puts his phone in his pocket. "Tonight we're attending the annual Hope Gala, benefiting cancer research. Apparently I'm a gold-level sponsor."

"That's generous of you." I sidle up to him and thread my arms around his waist. "Do you give a lot to charity?"

"Tammi handles it," he says. "But yeah. I mean, fuck, I don't need all my money. I suppose it's the least I can do."

Suddenly I'm overcome with curiosity. "Jackson, can I ask you a personal question?"

He steps backward and arches an eyebrow at me. "Should I be worried?"

"No, I'm just wondering. I've never asked you about your money, but... Is that a weird thing to ask about?"

"It's not weird." He gets himself a glass of ice water from the fridge and takes a drink. "My dad expected me to follow in his footsteps and work with him at Bennett Enterprises. I wasn't interested in his plans, so I struck out on my own. Some of it was down to luck, really. I hit the right industry at the right time. I started a software development company not long after I got out of college. Four years later, I sold it for one point five billion."

I almost choke. "Did you say a billion?"

"Yeah." He's so casual about it, like that figure means nothing. "The product took off and my competitor wanted the tech behind it. That didn't all go to me, of course, but most of it did. So I started reinvesting. Now I buy up companies in trouble, turn them around, and sell them off. I keep a few. And once in a while I buy something that's more of a hobby, like the art gallery in Jetty Beach. I don't know what I need an art gallery for, but I'm glad as fuck I decided to buy it."

I laugh and lean into him. "What does your father think of all this? Since you decided not to follow his plans, I mean."

Jackson doesn't answer right away, and I start regretting the question. He takes another drink.

"I don't know what he thinks."

"I'm sorry, I shouldn't have asked."

He sets his water down and puts an arm around me. "It's okay. My dad and I have never gotten along. He disapproves of my life pretty heavily."

"That seems crazy. Look at this. What is there to disapprove of?"

"I think he wanted me to fail so I'd have to come crawling back to Chicago."

"That's shitty."

"I try not to let it bother me. He has my brother to be the golden boy. Those two deserve each other. Besides, I'm pretty sure my net worth is higher than his, and that's the best revenge."

Dennis returns, his arms overflowing with bags. "This way, sweetheart."

I start to follow Dennis, and Jackson smacks my ass. I glare at him.

Dennis is already laying dresses out on the bed. "I think this one, but what do you think?" He holds up a knee length red gown with a plunging neckline.

"It's beautiful."

"Now that I look at it next to you, I'm not so sure," he says. "What kind of bra do you have on?"

"Um." His question takes me aback, and I open my shirt to glance down. "It's, I don't know, black."

"Shirt off."

I glance behind me, looking for Jackson. He leans against the door frame and gives me an encouraging nod.

I peel off my shirt and Dennis turns me around in a circle.

"This dress won't work unless you want to go braless. Which is fine, you certainly have the boobs for it. But you know what, this isn't the one anyway."

He tosses the dress onto the bed and picks up another one. It's long and shimmering black, with a slit up one side. He holds it up in front of me.

"Oh, yes," Dennis says. "This might be the one."

He helps me into the dress and zips up the back. The straps are wide and the neckline dips low. It hugs my curves, but isn't too tight, and the slit goes high up my right thigh.

"What do you think?" Dennis asks.

Jackson puts a hand to his chin, and his eyes rove up and down. "This might be too good. She's supposed to stay dressed, and I'm not sure I can do that."

Dennis holds up a finger. "Wait until you see the shoes. Size seven, seven and a half?"

I nod.

"That's what I thought." He pulls a shoe box from a shopping bag and opens it, producing a pair of black heels, each with a tiny silver bow on the back.

Jackson groans. "Fuck, Dennis, I don't think we're going to make it to the venue."

Dennis flashes a grin. "I aim to please."

I slip the shoes on my feet. They're taller than I'm used to, but surprisingly comfortable. I look down and run my hands down my waist to my hips, then look up at Jackson. "Yes?"

"Oh, fuck yes," Jackson says.

"Don't undress her yet," Dennis says.

I move into the bathroom and look at myself in the full length mirror. This dress is absolutely magnificent. It makes me feel like a million dollars.

I grab my brush from the counter and run it through my hair, which looks so plain next to this incredible dress I'm wearing.

"Here," Dennis says, coming into the bathroom. "Bennett didn't give me time to get someone in here to do this right, but I'll put it up for you."

"We don't have much time, Dennis," Jackson says from the bedroom.

"I know, I know," he says.

In no time at all, Dennis has my hair swept up in a classy up-do. I feel a little bit like Audrey Hepburn. I put on a little more makeup, doing my best with what I brought with me. I never wear much, so I feel like my face is a bit plain compared to the rest of my ensemble. But it will have to do.

I emerge from the bathroom to find Jackson dressed in a sleek black tux with a bow tie. I look him up and down, licking my lips. I want to loosen that sexy tie and undo his buttons one by one.

The corner of his mouth turns up in that devilish grin. "You look good enough to eat."

"You're not so bad yourself, captain."

"None of that," Dennis says. "I have to get you out the door or Tammi will have my ass."

Jackson adjusts his jacket and holds out an arm, leading me into the elevator and down to the waiting limo.

"What time does this thing start?" I ask when we're settled in the car. We're dressed for evening, but it's barely one o'clock.

"I figure we'll be there by six," he says.

"Six? Where are we going?"

"L.A."

I stare at him. I have to stop doing that, but he keeps dropping bombshells on me. "As in, Los Angeles?"

"Yeah."

I laugh. I shouldn't be surprised.

"Is that a problem?" he asks, putting a hand on my thigh.

"No, I just assumed it was here."

"We have a private plane, so the trip will be more than comfortable. And we can stay as long as we'd like. I have a room booked, but if you'd rather, we can fly back tonight. I figure we can see how the evening goes. These things tend to be pretty dull, to be honest."

Dull is not how I would describe it.

We fly in a jet that makes his limo look plain by comparison. Another car is waiting to whisk us to the Ritz Carlton, where it looks like a scene from a movie premier. There's a fucking red carpet. The car pulls up, the driver opens the door, and a million flashes of light blind me.

Jackson warned me there would be cameras, but I'm not prepared for the assault. I keep a death grip on his hand while we walk through the crowd, petrified I'll stumble. We stop for more photos in front of a backdrop with the gala logo. Jackson keeps a hand on the small of my back, turning occasionally as photographers call his name. I smile, hoping terror doesn't show in my face.

The rest of the dinner is a whirlwind. Our table is front and center in the huge ballroom and it's all I can do not to gape. I recognize at least half the other guests—they are real fucking celebrities. Actors, media personalities, people I see on TV all the time. Surreal isn't even the word. I thought spending a week in a mansion on the beach was insane. This is downright ridiculous.

I keep waiting for someone to gently tap me on the shoulder and ask me to leave. I'm not just a fish out of water, I'm a fish in the soul-sucking vacuum of space. But the entire time, Jackson is there, his hand on my skin, keeping me steady.

After dinner, and a droning speech by someone I don't recognize, Jackson leans over and asks if I'm ready to leave. I'm so grateful, I almost collapse. He says his goodbyes to the others at our table, and leads me out to the waiting car.

I slump into the seat and close my eyes. "Oh my god, that was exhausting."

Jackson laughs. "Drink?"

"Make it plural."

He pulls out a bottle—I don't even care what it is—and pours. I slam the whole thing in one swallow and hold out the glass for a refill.

"What do you think?" he asks, pouring me another. "Back to Seattle, or drinks in L.A.? It's still early."

I think about it for a moment. I *am* tired, but now that we're out of the banquet, I feel a lot better. "Dennis did go to all this trouble. I'd hate to let this dress go to waste."

Jackson smiles. "So would I."

He directs the driver to an elegant cocktail bar somewhere downtown. The lights are low, and a buzz of conversation surrounds us. I order a martini—it feels like a martini kind of place—and Jackson sips a glass of Irish Whiskey. He runs a hand up the slit of my dress, caressing my thigh as we talk. People move around us, but they fall from my notice in the presence of those dazzling blue eyes and his strong hands.

His eyes keep flicking to the side, as if he's looking behind me.

"Is something wrong?" I ask.

"Asshole over there keeps trying to take a picture of you. Don't look. Keep facing me. We'll go."

I stand, grabbing my little clutch purse. Jackson moves so he's standing between me and the photographer and wraps a protective arm around my shoulders.

A waiter comes near and speaks quiet words to Jackson, then walks away.

He takes off his coat and helps me slide my arms through. "There's more outside. They must have followed us from the hotel. We'll wait until the car is out front."

"Are you serious?"

"Yeah. They're like fucking rats. One shows up and starts attracting more. They all want to see what the story is, and be the one to get the winning shot." His phone lights up and he puts a hand on my back. "The car's here. Walk to the car, and get inside. You don't have to look at them or answer their questions."

My heart quickens, and nervousness runs through my belly. This is so bizarre.

We walk through the lobby and the host opens the door for us. Flashes go off and a press of people surge forward.

"Jackson, is this your mystery woman?"

"Jackson, is this your new girlfriend?"

"Can we get a shot of you with sassy girl?"

"Sassy girl, what's your name?"

"Who is she?"

Jackson keeps his arm tight around me. The few feet from the door to the edge of the sidewalk feel like a mile.

The driver helps me in and I scoot across the seat. Jackson follows and the door shuts, cameras still flashing outside the car.

"Fuck." He puts a hand over his mouth and looks out the window, his brow furrowed.

"What the hell was that?"

He doesn't answer—just stares out the window. The car pulls away and I shift in my seat, hugging his coat around me.

"Does that happen to you often?"

"It's been a while since they were interested enough to follow me around." He pauses again for a long moment, the lines of his jaw tight. "It's because of you."

"Me?"

"Because of me tweeting about you," he says. "I'm sorry, Melissa, I should have been prepared for that. I would have brought security if I'd known. We'll fly back tonight. Seattle won't be as bad."

"Are you sure?"

He looks away and gets on his phone. I hear things like *security*, *privacy*, and *keep the fuckers off my property*.

I'm just glad it's over.

20

MELISSA

We arrive back at Jackson's condo in the early hours of the morning. No photographers are waiting outside, so either they aren't following him in Seattle, or his angry phone calls did the trick and someone chased them off. A man in a dark suit stands in the lobby. I don't remember seeing security in Jackson's building before, but the man's presence makes me feel better. We crash out in the king-sized bed and enjoy a leisurely morning, sipping coffee on his balcony and enjoying the view.

I stay another night—there doesn't seem to be any reason to leave. In the morning, I wake to his voice through the closed bedroom door. He sounds angry.

Dressed in one of Jackson's t-shirts, I creep out of the bedroom and go to the kitchen to make coffee. He's pacing up and down the balcony, his movements controlled, but he's clearly agitated. His voice rises again and he hangs up, pocketing his phone.

"Everything okay?" I ask when he comes inside.

"Not really. I have to fly to fucking St. Louis."

"When?"

"In a couple hours."

My heart sinks. "How long will you be there?"

"A few days, probably. I have to go bust some heads before things get worse." He runs his hands up and down my arms. "I can have my driver take you home. Or you can stay here if you want."

I glance around. I don't feel comfortable staying at Jackson's place without him. "Thanks, but I think I'll go home."

"Yeah, of course."

Does he look disappointed?

He steps in, leans his head down to my hair, and takes a deep breath. His hands slide around my waist and he presses my body close.

"I don't want to go," he says into my ear.

His hand runs down my back and slips beneath my panties, grabbing my ass.

"How long do we have?" I ask, grabbing his cock through his pants.

He groans. "Long enough."

HIS DRIVER TAKES me home that afternoon. I call Nicole on the way and tell her about the craziness of the paparazzi. She can't believe it, and quite honestly, neither can I. It feels like something I read about happening to another person. They can't have been trying to take pictures of me.

As we drive into town, the familiarity of Jetty Beach is an enormous relief. It's a place where things don't change very much, and I need my hometown's solid ground beneath my feet.

My stomach drops when we turn onto my street. Cars are parked outside my house, lining the street on both sides.

People get out as soon as the driver pulls up. They're all holding up cameras.

The glass partition lowers and the driver turns around. "I'll get you inside your house, okay?"

I swallow hard and nod. I send a quick text to Jackson, although I know there's nothing he can do. He's probably in the air, on his way to St. Louis.

Paparazzi outside my house. WTF.

The driver opens my door. I slip a pair of sunglasses on my face and grab my bag. He puts an arm around my shoulders and guides me toward my front door, amid at least a dozen people with cameras trying to get close.

"Melissa, are you Jackson Bennett's infamous sassy girl?"

"Melissa, look at me!"

"Melissa, how does it feel to be Jackson Bennett's flavor of the month?"

"Melissa, how does a small-town girl nab the most eligible bachelor in the country?"

"Melissa!"

I bite my lip to keep from yelling obscenities at them. The driver stands close behind me while I fumble with my keys. He nudges me inside and closes the door. I turn to find him gone, already making his way back to the car. No one followed up to my porch, but they all linger outside on the path from the sidewalk. I quickly shut the curtains and retreat to my bedroom.

My phone rings. Jackson.

"Hi."

"Don't go in," he says, his voice urgent. "I'll get you a hotel."

"I already did. Your driver was really nice. He helped me to my front door."

"Fuck. How many are there?"

"A dozen, maybe? I didn't stop to count."

"Son of a bitch. Listen, don't go anywhere. I'm arranging for private security, but no one can get to you for a couple of hours."

"Private security? Jackson, this is insane."

"I know." There's so much rage in his voice, it scares me. "Just, stay where you are. I can't get there right now, but... fuck. You know what, I'm sending my driver back. He'll take you back to my place. I don't want you there alone."

"What? No, I just got home. They'll get bored and leave."

"No, they won't. You're not staying there by yourself."

"Jackson, this is my home. They aren't going to chase me out of my own house, and you don't get to order me around."

"This isn't optional, Melissa. I can't... Fuck, I can't be there right now, and I don't want you there by yourself. Please, let me get you somewhere safe."

"Safe? They have cameras, not handguns. I'm fine. I don't know how I'm going to go to the fucking store later, but I'm fine."

"Goddammit, Melissa, don't go to the store. Fuck it. I'm coming back."

"No," I say, my voice emphatic. "No, you're not coming here. You have shit to do, and it's a lot more important than a bunch of douchenozzles camped out on my front lawn."

"It's not more important."

I slump, putting a hand to my forehead. "Will you go to your meetings if I get a hotel?"

"Yes, but don't go anywhere yet. Wait for Curt."

"Who is Curt?"

"Security. He'll get you where you need to go safely. What hotel do you want?"

"I... I have no idea."

"Don't worry about it. Tammi will text you. Just, fuck, don't move. Wait for Curt, okay? He'll be there in a couple of hours."

"Jackson, seriously, I don't think these photographers are going to hurt me."

"They better not lay a finger on you or I'll rip their fucking throats out."

His voice is so cold, I have no doubt he's serious. It sends a shiver up my spine.

"Okay, it's fine. I'll wait here for Curt. I'll watch *Firefly* or something."

"Promise?"

"Yes, I promise."

"Close the curtains and lock all the doors."

"I already did."

"All right," he says, his voice softer. "I'll take care of things out here and I'll come back as soon as I can. If things get worse, Curt will take you to my place. Fuck, I wish you'd just go, I'd feel better with you there."

"Jackson, I'm fine."

"Okay, baby. I—" He hesitates. "I'll call you in a little while."

He hangs up, and I let the phone drop to the bed. What the fuck is happening? Do I actually have paparazzi outside my house? This cannot be real. I'm no one. Just a girl from Jetty Beach who stumbled into a world where I do not belong.

I lie down, letting my head hit the pillow. This is his world, his life. Black tie galas and photographers and celebrities. Part of me desperately wishes he was here, but another part wonders what the fuck I'm doing. I'm waiting for private security to whisk me off to a hotel. I can't even stay in my own house.

My private moments with Jackson have been amazing and wonderful, but that's only one part of his life. This—the chaos, the questions, the pictures—is as much a part of his life as the rest of it.

I don't think I can handle it.

21

JACKSON

The crisis in St. Louis takes four days to fix. I spend the entire trip worried out of my mind for Melissa. She assures me she's fine, and I check in with her security multiple times a day. Maybe I'm acting like a lunatic, but I don't give a shit. It's killing me that she's thousands of miles away and I can't be there to keep her safe. The entire thing is my fault.

I stopped tweeting about her after San Diego, but the damage was done. I turned her into a mystery, and once it caught the attention of the gossip writers, it was over. They had to know who she was. And of course, they found her.

I've had plenty of run-ins with paparazzi over the years. Occasionally something stirs them up, and I'll find them outside my building. Once a guy sneaked into one of my parties and I had to have him forcibly removed. In the past, I'd tighten my security for a while, or maybe disappear in the middle of the night to some random city. The attention dies down and they move on to someone else. Life goes on.

But knowing they're camped outside Melissa's house makes me panic. I almost fired my driver for leaving her, but it turned out he parked his car up the street and waited, watching her house until Curt arrived. Sending her to a hotel is better than having her stay at home, but I wish she'd go to my place—I can lock that place down like a bunker. But when I bring it up again the next day, it only makes her mad.

In fact, she sounds mad every time I talk to her, but I'm not sure what else I can do.

After one final morning meeting, I fly back to Seattle. I have the Bugatti brought to the airport—I'll probably get pulled over ten times on the drive down, but fuck it, I don't care. There are still a hundred fifty miles between us, and I'm determined to get to her.

I check in with her security when I get close to town. I'm livid when Curt tells me she isn't at the hotel, so I drive to her house. A few cars are still parked on the street, and I notice another following me. I pull up to her house and get out, ignoring the assholes who lean out of their car windows to take pictures. They're lucky they don't rush me. I'll hit the first person to get near me, I'm so pissed.

Curt lets me in, and I find Melissa sitting at her kitchen table. The curtains are all drawn and she has blankets up over the windows.

"What the fuck are you doing here?"

Her mouth drops open and she lets the pen she's holding drop. "Excuse me? I'm fine, thank you. Nice to see you."

"You were supposed to stay at the hotel."

"What the fuck was I supposed to do sitting in a goddamn hotel room for days on end?" she asks. "Sit around ordering room service? Watch some porn?"

"Those assholes are still out there."

"Oh, you noticed that? Thank you for pointing out the

obvious, because here I was, thinking they'd gone and I could go back to my fucking life."

I put my hands in my pockets and take a deep breath. This is not going the way it is supposed to. "I'm sorry this happened. I know you're mad. I deserve it. This was my fault. I wasn't prepared, and I should have been."

"How do you prepare for something like this? Every time I leave, I have to wear sunglasses and a hoodie. It got worse before it got better, you know. Today there's only a few of them left, but two days ago? The hotel called the police, so they just started hanging out around town. I don't even know how many of them were here. I guess some of them got bored, because by the time I came home there weren't as many people following me."

"Why did you come back here?"

"Because sitting in a hotel room with Curt was fucking miserable." She leans toward the doorway. "No offense, Curt, you're super nice."

"None taken, Mel," Curt says from the other room.

"Damn it, Melissa, you're right on the ground floor. They could—"

"What, peek in my windows? Because they did that. Knock on my door at six in the morning? Yeah, they did that too. Follow me around town? Yep. Every time."

"That's why I told you to go to my place." I'm so exasperated. What part of this does she not understand?

"As if that would have mattered."

"Of course it would have mattered. They can wander around my building all they want. You'd be safe upstairs."

"No, it doesn't even fucking matter." She taps furiously on her laptop. "Did you see this bullshit?"

She turns the screen around. It's some celebrity gossip website. The headline reads, *Jackson Bennett Mystery Solved.*

Below is a picture of us in the club in San Diego. I have my hands all over her ass, and my face in her neck. She looks drunk. It isn't a flattering shot.

"Listen to this," she says, turning her laptop back around. "Jackson Bennett, playboy billionaire, had the Twitter-verse aflutter with his cryptic tweets and photos of an unknown woman. Who was this girl who had captured the heart of the notorious bachelor? She's none other than Melissa Simon, a fifth-grade teacher from a small town on the Washington coast. How did an ordinary girl snag the most eligible man in America? Judging by their wild excursions, we can certainly imagine." She pauses, scrolling with her mouse. "And look at this, there's us on the beach in San Diego, and you have your hand up my dress. And here we are at the club again, this time with my ass in your groin. That's lovely. I certainly don't look like a cheap whore. Oh, look, they decided to bury the one decent picture of us at the stupid banquet at the bottom. That's great." Her voice is thick with sarcasm.

"Yeah, it sucks when they do that, but this will all blow over in a week or so."

"Is that what you think?" she asks, slamming her laptop closed. "Because I don't think this is going to blow anywhere. Do you want to know why I know about this article, and these photos? My boss, Jackson. My motherfucking boss called me this morning. He said he's *concerned.* He wonders whether I'm in the right profession, based on my *extracurricular activities.* I'm union, so it won't be easy to fire me, but he can make my life miserable in the meantime. As soon as this gets around town, I'm screwed. Parents are going to call the district, demanding I be let go. They won't want their kids around *that.*" She gestures to her laptop. "I can do what I want on my own time, but I can't have it splashed across the internet for everyone to see. They'll probably force me to resign."

"They can't do that."

"Believe me, they can."

I put a hand to my mouth and turn away. How did this turn into such a disaster?

Melissa gets up and storms off to her bedroom. I follow her down the hall and close the door behind me.

"What do you want me to do? I'll fix this."

She whirls around. "How will you fix this? Tell me. Will you call my boss and convince him that I'm not some groupie? Explain to the parents of my students that it isn't as bad as it looks in the pictures? That I'm still the same Ms. Simon they've been trusting with their kids for years? Maybe you can buy them off. Make a big donation to the school, and then they'll make this all go away."

It isn't a bad idea. I open my mouth, but she keeps talking.

"No, do not even say it. Your money can't fix this."

I stare at her, my mouth still open, the words I was about to say retreating into the sudden silence. Her eyes are wet with tears and she swallows hard.

"It should have just been a week," she says. "That was the deal."

I stagger backward and clutch my chest, like she hit me. "What is that supposed to mean?"

"Did you think this could work beyond that? I don't understand this world that you live in. It isn't my world. I don't belong in it any more than you belong out here. I can't figure out how to make this work. You have private jets and parties and paparazzi. But I have a life, too. You can't just swoop in here in a limo and make all my problems go away."

"That's not what I'm trying to do."

"We aren't doing ourselves any favors by dragging this out." Tears roll down her cheeks. "We both know how this ends. This can't work. We're too different." She pauses again and turns away from me. "I think you should just go."

I look down at the floor, my chest tightening. What is happening? Why the fuck do I care so much? I've known her for what, a little over a month? Maybe she's right. Half the things I do confuse her. I never wanted a relationship anyway. It was only supposed to last a week.

"Fine. Curt will stay until the paparazzi leave for good. I won't bother you again."

I leave her room and walk out the front door.

22

JACKSON

I wander through the party on the first floor of my condo. People laugh, smile, hold up their drinks to toast me. I clutch a glass of Scotch in my hand and half nod at the people I pass. It's a great party—Dennis outdid himself. Music blares through the speakers; a bartender spins bottles, earning cheers from my guests; and beautiful women are everywhere. It isn't even a weekend, and my place is packed.

None of it makes me feel better.

I barely remember the drive home from the beach last week. I was in a haze of anger and hurt. I don't need all this fucking drama. Melissa was right: We said a week and we should have left it at that. It was a fantastic week—I think even she agrees with me there—but it's over. I had my fun, and I need to go back to my life.

Then why does my life seem so fucking empty?

I pull out my phone and unlock the door to my private stairwell. Someone calls my name, but I ignore them. The bass bumps through the wall as I walk up the stairs to the top floor. I thought having my condo full of people would help. It's what I do; I love to drink and dance and flirt and get lucky, all to blow off steam. My daily life is full of pressure—I need an outlet.

Why is losing Melissa any different? I have deals go south all the time. I've left women behind. None of it fazes me. I party it up and get back to work in the morning.

But a week has gone by since I left her, and nothing is the same.

I set my untouched drink on the kitchen counter. I feel like shit, and I have no idea what to do about it. I drank myself into a stupor after I got back from her house, but all that gained me was a fucking hangover. I go to the office, staying late every day. But I still come home to a bunch of empty rooms and a hole in my chest that nothing can fill.

The door opens and I glance up. Tammi walks in, still dressed for business, even though it's after ten o'clock.

"Evening." She pulls up a bar stool and sets a file folder down on the counter. "I couldn't find you downstairs, but someone said they saw you come up here. That's quite the party you have going down there."

"Yeah, I guess. What are you doing here?"

"I need a signature," she says, pushing the file toward me. "They Fed Exed the contract from St. Louis this afternoon and if you sign everything now, I can send it off in the morning. I'm supposed to be out of the office tomorrow."

"Out of the office?" I ask, sliding the file around so I can see it.

"Yes. You *are* legally obligated to give me a day off once in a while, you know."

"I know. What are you doing with your day out of the office?"

Her brows crease, like she's surprised at my question. "Well, my husband and I are going out of town for the weekend. You can still text me if you need something, but I might need a grace period before I respond."

"No, it's fine," I say, flipping through the pages of the contract. "I won't bother you."

"Are you drunk? Because if you're drunk, I can't notarize this."

I nod toward my glass. "That's my first, and I haven't touched it yet." I thought I wanted a Scotch, but I can't bring myself to drink it. I find a pen and sign where Tammi placed Post-its. "That it?"

"Yes, but..." She hesitates. "Are you okay?"

I look away. "No."

"Oh. I didn't expect you to say that."

I rub my chin and let out a breath. "Tammi, I don't know what the fuck is wrong with me."

"Is it about Melissa?"

"Yeah, she's ... she doesn't want to see me."

"What happened?"

"A bunch of dipshits with cameras found her. They camped outside her house and followed her around town when I was in St. Louis. Then they printed a bunch of bullshit online and her boss saw it, so now she's worried about her job—or she was a week ago. I haven't talked to her. She told me to leave, so I did. I don't know why I'm telling you all of this."

"Wow," Tammi says.

"What does that mean?"

"I just ... I didn't think it was possible."

I sigh. "What?"

"You're in love with her."

I stare at her, stunned. It's like she hit me upside the head with a two by four.

"What the fuck did you just say?"

The corners of her mouth turn up in a smile. "You're in love with Melissa. That's what's been going on this whole time."

Oh, hell no. I do *not* do the L-word. I don't love anyone, except maybe myself. But a woman? No. It isn't going to happen.

Except…

"Well, if being in love feels like my chest is going to cave in, then maybe I am."

"That's exactly what it feels like." Her voice is sort of awed.

"Fuck off."

"Don't talk to me like that," she says with a roll of her eyes. "And yes, it does. When you're with her, you feel like your whole world is complete. Like you can't fathom the idea of spending another minute apart. And when you're not together, you think about her constantly. Like she took a piece of you with her. There's a space only she can fill."

I pick up my drink and toss the whole thing back in one swallow. *In love?* No fucking way. But Tammi's making a little too much sense. "I feel like I'm dying. Like I'm going to suffocate. Is that love? Because if it is, it fucking sucks."

Tammi laughs. "Yeah, especially when things are uncertain. Come on, Jackson, you can't tell me you had no idea. You've been insane for her since you met her. Even I could see it."

I grab a bottle—I don't even look to see what it is—and pour another drink. "Yeah, sure, she's great. She's beautiful and fun, and fucking incredible. Anyone would think that. It has nothing to do with being in love."

"No, that's all being in love."

I pause, sipping from my glass. I can't taste it.

Dennis walks in, and I almost tell him to leave. I'm confused as hell and I'm pretty sure he isn't going to help.

"Is there a problem? You disappeared. People are asking for you."

"I'm done for tonight."

Tammi rotates on her stool. "He's in love with Melissa."

"Yeah, I know that," Dennis says.

My mouth drops open.

"See?" Tammi says.

"Don't start ganging up on me," I say. "Why are we talking about this?"

"Did you break up with that sweet woman?" Dennis says. "Is that why you've been moping around all week?"

"I have not been moping. And no, *she* asked *me* to leave."

"Damn," Dennis says. He shares a look with Tammi.

"Will you two stop that. I'll fire you both."

"Can I just speak plainly?" Tammi asks.

"As opposed to the way you usually speak?"

She raises an eyebrow. "You are who you are. You've lived this way for a long time, and probably been through a lot of women. Melissa was different from the beginning, though, wasn't she? You care about her. You want her in your life. Am I wrong?"

"No."

"Then stop sulking," she says. "Tell her."

I take another sip. "That's the thing. She doesn't want me."

"Are you sure about that?" Tammi asks.

"Yeah, she made it pretty fucking clear."

"Well I saw the two of you together, and I could see it," Dennis says. "You love her, and I'm telling you, she loves you, too."

"If she does—and I'm not saying she does—it isn't enough."

"He's really pathetic, isn't he?" Dennis says.

Tammi nods. "I know."

"Seriously? Fucking fired. Both of you."

"Maybe she just needs a little time," Tammi says, completely ignoring me. "You do have a tendency to live like you're the center of a whirlwind. It can be overwhelming."

I think about our trip to San Diego. The airport. First class. The villa. "Yeah, I was good at overwhelming her."

"Listen, you want my advice?" Tammi asks.

"No."

"Give her a little space. Let things cool down, and then call her."

"Tammi's right," Dennis says, leaning against the counter.

"I'm just so damn worried about her. She made Curt leave yesterday. She's out there all by herself."

"She's a grown woman," Tammi says. "She handled herself just fine before you swooped into her life. I'm pretty sure she'll be okay. I know patience isn't one of your virtues, but try it this time. Be patient with her. She'll talk to you when she's ready."

"Sure, fine," I say. "Now both of you, get the fuck out of here, or I'm definitely firing you."

They share another infuriating smile and leave.

Love? I've never been in love. Is that what this horrible ache is? Why would anyone want to feel like this? Life was a hell of a lot easier before I met her. But as shitty as I feel, I can't regret it. I just don't know what I'm going to do about it.

I found the one thing I want that my money can't buy.

23

MELISSA

Adjusting to my life post-Jackson isn't much fun. I box up all the clothes he bought for me and tuck them away in a closet. Even the shoes—especially the shoes. I hang out with friends, read books I can't remember as soon as I finish them, and tinker with things around my house. Anything to fill my time and keep my mind off him.

The paparazzi eventually go away. They hang around town for a while, but news seems to get out that I'm no longer Jackson's latest plaything. A few days later, they're nowhere to be seen, and I insist that Curt and his cohorts go home. They're nice guys, and they've only been doing their job, but their presence is suffocating. I feel like a prisoner in my own home. I can't live like that.

I'm still not sure how things will shake out at work. I need to meet with my boss face to face to discuss what happened. I send him a long email, explaining as best I can—how the media chose the worst pictures. How I was on vacation with a friend, and he happened to be well-known. That I didn't actually do anything wrong, other than be photographed with a public figure.

He sends me a response that seems positive, but it's hard to tell what the true consequences will be. I hate the thought of losing my job. But at the same time, if I can't feel free to be myself when I'm on my own time, I'm not sure I want to deal with that.

It calls into question everything I've planned for my future—but I decide that maybe that isn't such a bad thing. I'll live with a little uncertainty for a while, and decide what the best course of action is when things calm down. At least there won't be any more photos of me circulating online.

I try to tell myself I did the right thing. Jackson and I are so different. It doesn't make sense to keep seeing each other if we have no future. But the pain in my chest doesn't go away. Not the first day, nor the second. A week goes by and I still feel awful. I start to wonder if I'm ever going to get over him. Even the guy I dated for two years just after college didn't mess me up so badly. I missed him when we decided to part ways, but for the most part, I just went on with my life. I was sad, but nothing like this.

It doesn't make any sense.

I wake up on a Wednesday morning and realize I'm out of coffee. That shit isn't going to fly, and I'm out of other things as well, so I run to the store. I pick up some staples and when I come home, I turn on the TV, just for the background noise.

I open the cupboard in the bathroom to put away a package of toilet paper, and notice an unopened box of tampons. When did I buy those? And why are they still unopened?

My hands shake and I close the cupboard door. There is no way.

I start doing the math in my head. When did I last have a

period? How long ago was it that I met Jackson? When were we in San Diego? What day is it?

I grab my phone and open the calendar. I definitely wasn't on my period in San Diego. Nor the couple of weeks before. In fact, my last period ended the day before I met Jackson at Danny's. I remember because when he told me I was coming back to his hotel with him, the thought went through my head: *my period is over, so maybe...*

How long ago was that?

I flip through the calendar and start counting. I get to twenty-eight and keep going. Holy shit. Thirty. Thirty-five. Forty. Forty-five. Fifty.

Fifty-one.

My last period started fifty-one fucking days ago? How the hell did I not realize?

I don't generally keep careful track of my cycles. I'm as regular as clockwork, and good about remembering to keep tampons in my purse, so it never catches me off guard. It starts, I cope with it, no big deal. I don't think about it much in between.

The last couple months have been so damn crazy that I haven't even thought about my cycle. But there's no way I can deny it. I'm late. Really late.

Fucking hell.

I sit down on the couch, wondering what I should do. I think about calling Nicole, but I don't want to freak her out unnecessarily. I slide my laptop over and Google *reasons for a late period*.

Stress. Yes, stress is a reason my period could be late. Could that make it *this* late? I have no idea, but I've been under plenty of stress. Maybe this thing with Jackson messed with me more than I realized. I believe in that whole mind-body connection stuff. I've been through a lot, so maybe my hormones are simply screwed up.

I put a hand on my belly. Shouldn't I feel something? I Google again, looking for pregnancy symptoms. I'm not nauseated. I press my hands against my boobs—no soreness. I'm not sensitive to smells, and food tastes the same. No cramping, no unexplained back aches. No cravings. I go down the list and can honestly say I feel none of it. I have no symptoms.

I blow out a breath, trying to ignore the line at the bottom of the page that says, *Some women don't experience symptoms in early pregnancy, so the presence or absence of any of these is not a reliable indicator*.

What the fuck am I supposed to do now? I grab my phone and sling my purse over my shoulder, heading out to my truck. I can't sit around and wait for my period to start. Not knowing will drive me crazy, and at this point I'm late enough it doesn't make sense to take the *wait and see* approach. I need to get a test.

But there's no way I'm going to buy a home pregnancy test at Charlie's Grocery. I know everyone who works there. And the gas station is out; I know everyone there, too. With everything that's happened recently, I do not need rumors going around town about Melissa Simon buying pregnancy tests. Especially if I'm not actually pregnant—which I definitely am not. I just need to see the negative on a test. Then I'll be sure, and I can stop worrying.

I drive forty-five minutes to another town. I wander through the grocery store, half-filling a cart with bullshit I don't need, just so I won't be buying nothing but a bunch of pregnancy tests. In the aisle of terror, I stare at the options. They're right next to the condoms and lube, across the aisle from all the feminine hygiene stuff. Interesting placement. I have no idea which one to buy, so I get several of each brand. Maybe one is better than the others, and if the test isn't clear, I want to be able to take another one. I am *not* coming back to the store to buy more.

At the checkout counter, I'm sure the cashier can hear my heart racing. It feels like it's going to beat out of my chest. I keep my sunglasses on, and thumb through a magazine, trying to avoid meeting the woman's eye. She doesn't say anything past the usual niceties. I pay and get myself out of there as quickly as I can.

The drive home is agony. Why did I go so far? It's the stupidest thing, to drive two towns away just to go to the damn store. The gas gauge on my truck is dangerously low, and I squeeze the steering wheel, hoping the gas light won't go on. I don't want to stop. I'm trembling with nervousness and feel sick to my stomach. Fuck, is that a pregnancy thing? Or am I just scared?

When I get home, I bring the bags in and run to the bathroom. I need to pee something fierce, but I've been holding it, knowing I'll need it for the test.

With my stomach still roiling, I take out one of the tests. I make myself breathe and read the instructions. It's pretty straightforward. Take off the protective cover. Place in urine stream. Set face up on the counter or other flat surface. Wait three minutes.

I follow the instructions, leave it sitting on the counter, and set a timer on my phone. I can't bear to wait in the same room, so I wash my hands and pace through my house. It's the longest three minutes of my life.

My phone dings and it feels like my heart stops. It will be negative. It has to be negative. We used protection. I don't want to think about the whole *not one hundred percent* bullshit they put on condom boxes. I need to go look. My fears will be put to rest, and I can call Nicole and tell her what a psycho I've been. She'll get a great laugh out of the whole thing.

I creep into the bathroom, my hand covering my eyes, like I'm watching a horror movie and I'm too scared to look. The test is supposed to be easy to read, with either a big *Pregnant* or *Not Pregnant* showing in the display window. I part my fingers, peering down at the test, and almost throw up.

Pregnant.

24

MELISSA

I sit on the exam table, the sheet of white paper crinkling beneath me. My stomach is sour—whether from nerves or the baby making its presence known, I can't tell. I bounce my heel against the side of the table and fidget, wringing my hands in my lap. I've never been so terrified in my entire life.

After taking my vitals and having the gall to make me step on a scale, the nurse left me in the room, letting me know the doctor would be in shortly. I don't bother to correct her. I'm not here to see the doctor; I'm here to see the nurse practitioner. I asked for Addy specifically. She's who I see regularly. I've known her a long time, and I know she'll be straight with me.

The door opens and my mouth drops open. "Fucking hell."

Cody glances up from his clipboard and his brow furrows. "Oh, hey, Melissa." He comes in and shuts the door behind him. "Sorry, I hadn't looked at the name. I didn't realize it was you."

"I made an appointment with Addy Martin. Not with you."

"Addy's home with the flu, so I'm covering her patients. I'm sorry, the front desk should have told you."

"They didn't."

Cody takes a deep breath. He's in a blue-on-blue button-down shirt and tie, with a pair of khaki slacks. "Do you want to reschedule?"

Cody isn't a bad guy. But this is not the sort of thing you want to discuss with your best friend's fiancé's brother. Plus, I've known Cody since we were kids. It's so awkward.

But since I'm already here. "No," I say, slumping down a little. "It's fine."

"Okay." He sits down on the round rolling stool, facing me. "What's going on?"

"Can you tell me if all these could be false positives?" I pull out a plastic shopping bag full of pregnancy tests.

Cody raises his eyebrows and looks in the bag, shifting the contents around to see what's inside.

"How many?"

"I don't know. A dozen?"

"All positive?"

"Yep."

He hands the bag back to me. "Yeah, those don't really give false positives. You might get a false negative if you test too early, but once you're far enough along, the test will pick up the hCG. There's not a reason to have hCG in your system other than pregnancy."

I stare at the bag. I know he's right. I understand the biology. I'd hoped I missed something, that I was wrong about how they work and I screwed up when I took the tests. All twelve of them.

"If you want, I can do another test here, but it's basically the same as the ones you've already taken. The tests on the market are just as sensitive as the ones we use here. But if you want to go pee in a cup..."

"No, I think it's pretty clear."

"Do you want to talk about your options?"

I'm still half mortified to be sitting in a doctor's office with Cody as the doctor, but his voice has so much compassion.

"No, I understand my options."

"Okay. If you decide to proceed with the pregnancy, I do obstetrics—but I can refer you to someone else if that would be more comfortable for you."

"Yeah, I'm not sure I want you getting that familiar with my vagina."

Cody laughs. "Fair enough. If you want to see me for your first couple prenatal appointments, we can leave your vagina out of it entirely. Mostly we'll just need to check on you periodically to see how things are progressing, and I usually order blood work around twelve weeks. You get to keep your pants on for all of that."

"Thanks, Cody. Or, you know, Dr. Jacobsen."

He shakes his head. "Cody. And listen, this might go without saying, but I'll say it anyway: Whatever happens here, stays here. It's like Vegas, only with stethoscopes and tongue depressors. You don't have to worry about me saying anything, to anyone."

"Thank you."

"Now for a question from me as Cody, not as your doctor."

"Sure."

"Are you okay?"

"Honestly? No. I'm very much not okay. But I'll figure this out."

"Yeah, you will. Let me know if there's anything else I can do, okay? I mean that."

"Thank you. Really. I appreciate that."

"You bet. I have some brochures and things, if you'd like."

"That's okay."

He stands. "I'll let you get out of here, then. Just give us a call when you're ready to make an appointment, or let us know if you'd like a referral somewhere else."

"I will."

Cody leaves, and I pull out my phone. If this is really happening, I can't face it alone. I tap out a text to Nicole. *Are you busy? Can you meet me at my place? Important.*

Seconds later, my phone buzzes with her reply. *On my way.*

I tuck my phone back into my purse and grab my bag of doom. Shit is getting awfully real.

NICOLE LIVES twenty minutes north of town, so she arrives about fifteen minutes after I get home from the doctor's office. She bursts in without knocking.

"What's going on? Did you hear from Jackson?"

"No."

"Is it your dad?"

"No, Dad's okay." I'm not sure how to tell her this. She's my best friend, but I suddenly have the horrible fear that she's going to be disappointed in me.

I sink down on the couch and pull a pillow onto my lap. Nicole sits down beside me.

"Then what is it?" she asks.

"I'm pregnant."

Nicole is silent for a long moment, staring at me. "I'm sorry, what?"

"You heard me. Knocked up."

"You're sure? How many times have you tested?"

I grab the shopping bag and hand it to her.

She pulls apart the edges and looks in, the plastic crinkling. "Okay. That's ... yeah."

"I just got back from the doctor's office. It was fucking *Cody*, though. That was awesome. And by awesome, I mean mortifying."

"Oh my god, you saw Cody?" She puts a hand to her mouth, clearly trying to stifle laughter.

I glare at her. "It's not funny."

"No, no, it isn't," she says, still half laughing. "It's just ... of course you'd go to the doctor and it would be Cody."

"I made the appointment to see someone else, but she wasn't there."

"Yeah, at least Cody's a good guy. Okay, so you're pregnant. Holy shit, Melissa. This is huge."

"You think?"

"Do you know why it happened? What were you using?"

"Just condoms. But we used one every single time. Every time, I swear. We went through a lot of them."

"Well, they're not one hundred percent. Nothing is."

A memory runs through my mind, hazy with alcohol. "Oh shit."

"What?"

"The limo."

"What about the limo?

"We went out to this club and got really drunk, and then he fucked me in the limo. And again in the villa. I have no idea if he used a condom. And—son of a bitch—the time he showed up here in the middle of the night. He might not have then, either. I was half asleep, I didn't even think about it."

"Well, I guess that would do it." She's quiet for a long moment. "Have you told him?"

I stare at my coffee table. When I answer, my voice trembles. "No. I haven't talked to him at all."

"Come here, sweetie," she says, wrapping her arms around me. I lean into her. "You know you have to tell him, right?"

I groan.

"It's his baby too, Mel. He has a right to know."

"There's no way he's going to want to have anything to do with this I know how he lives. His life is all parties and fancy restaurants and expensive clothes and yelling at people in meetings. There's no room for a baby in all that. I don't even think he wants kids."

"Do you know that? Did he ever say he doesn't want kids?"

"No. We never talked about it. Why would we? This wasn't supposed to happen. We were supposed to go off and have this crazy week that didn't mean anything."

Nicole leans her cheek against my head. "But it did mean something, didn't it?"

Tears sting my eyes. "Yeah. It did."

NICOLE MAKES tea and stays with me for a while. It's well after dark when she finally leaves. She offers to stay over, but I don't want to make her do that. It isn't like it will change anything.

And there's a phone call I need to make.

Dread makes my fingers jittery as I bring up Jackson's

number. I do not want to do this. But I have to. There isn't any other option. My heart beats hard, and I feel a bit like I might throw up. I figure I should get used to that feeling.

He answers on the first ring. "Hi, Melissa?"

The background is so loud, I almost can't hear him. "Hi, yeah. I can't hear you very well."

"Sorry. Hold on." He pauses and the noise fades. "There, is that better?"

"Now you sound kind of echoey."

"I'm in the stairwell."

"Of your building? What's going on?"

"Um, nothing, just, you know, some people."

"Oh, right, a party. Fuck, it's Friday night. I didn't even think of that."

"No, it's okay," he says. "Don't apologize. It's good to hear your voice. Really good."

"Listen, Jackson, I need to talk to you about something."

"Yeah, me too. I've been wanting to talk to you but—"

"Jackson. Please let me talk."

"Sure."

I take a deep breath. *There's only one way to say this.* "I'm pregnant."

Jackson is silent. I wait, bile rising in my throat.

"Jackson?"

"You ... okay ... um."

The phone disconnects.

He fucking hung up on me? Anger tears through me and I almost throw my phone at the wall. That fucking bastard. He gets me pregnant and now he can't even—

My phone rings. Jackson.

I press answer, ready to fly off the handle and scream at him.

"Melissa? Please, I'm sorry. I dropped my phone. I swear, I didn't mean to hang up."

I hold the phone to my ear, breathing hard.

"Melissa? I'm sorry, I just didn't expect that. You took me by surprise."

"Yeah, it took me by surprise, too."

"Holy shit. Okay, I'm... Sorry, I'm just not sure what to say."

"You don't have to say anything. I will. This happened. I'm pregnant. And I'm going to have the baby, so let's not even talk about that. That's just how it's going to be. I'm sure this is something you've tried to avoid for a long time. It sucks that it had to be me. But I won't make a mess of this for you, okay? I'm not going to come after you, or broadcast this to the world or anything. I don't need anything from you. I felt like you had the right to know about it, but that's where this ends for you. You don't need to do anything."

"I don't need to do anything?" I can hear the anger in his voice. "Melissa, this is my baby, too. Of course I'm going to do something. What the fuck? Do you think I'd just walk away?"

"Well, look at you. You're probably half drunk at your party right now. This isn't what you wanted. You didn't want long-term. You wanted a fun time with me, and you got it."

"Is that what you think?" he says. "That's all it was?"

"We both know that's what it was." My throat feels like it's going to close up, and tears fill my eyes again.

"I'm not going to just walk away.

"You can't fix this, Jackson. Your money isn't going to help."

"Yes, it is. No, that's not what I mean. I can help with costs, obviously. That's a given, but that's not all I can do. I can be there. I want to."

"I won't be a responsibility that will wind up stifling you." I sniff and take a shuddering breath, trying to hold back the tears. "I called because you needed to know. That's all."

I hang up and toss my phone on the couch.

Seconds later, my phone buzzes, lighting up with Jackson's number. I don't answer. He knows. I did what I had to do. I can't talk to him anymore.

25

JACKSON

I hit send, trying to call Melissa again, but she doesn't answer. I don't bother leaving a message. I don't know what to say. I can't make her talk to me.

My chest is tight, like I can't breathe, and I stare at the wall. Did she just say she's pregnant? How is that possible? We were careful. I was...

Oh.

No, I wasn't careful. Not every time. After the club, I was too drunk to think straight. I remember hiking up her skirt in the limo, but I do not remember putting on a condom. And I can't blame the alcohol—that wasn't the only time. At her house, when I surprised her in the middle of the night. A voice in the back of my mind tried to remind me, but she felt so fucking good. I didn't stop myself. She didn't say anything either, but I certainly can't blame this on her. She was clear with me that she wasn't using birth control, and I said I'd take care of it.

Come to think of it, she's the only woman I've ever had unprotected sex with. I always use a condom, even when the woman assures me she's on birth control. I *never* take that chance. Too many women have tried to worm their way into my life over the years, wanting my money. An unplanned pregnancy is eighteen to life. I wasn't going to let a woman snare me that way.

I'm not even sure I want kids. I'm a great long-range planner when it comes to business, but as far as my personal life goes, I fly by the seat of my pants. Before meeting Melissa, I had no desire for a relationship, let alone a family. I saw the bullshit my parents went through. They were miserable. My own experiences with women were more or less the same. After a while, all my relationships went downhill, and I ended them. I'm resigned to being the perpetual bachelor. I have other things in my life that fulfill me.

I go upstairs, leaving the noise of the party behind. I'm not enjoying it anyway. Just a bunch of hangers-on, all wanting a piece of me. I don't know who half of them are. Maybe more than half. I keep trying to fill the quiet, to dull the pain in my gut, but nothing works. I don't want those assholes who are clogging up my condo, drinking my booze. I don't want another bottle of Scotch, or a new car, or a vacation in the fucking Caribbean—all things I would have turned to in the past when life got hard.

I want Melissa.

I grab a bottle of water out of my fridge and take a drink, trying to gather my thoughts. She's pregnant. Melissa is going to have a baby.

My baby.

That should terrify me. I should be calling Tammi—having her draw up some sort of agreement to make this go away. I'd agree to pay for everything if I can step out of the picture, and make Melissa sign something so she won't go to the media. I should be shaking with fear, or with anger, or … something.

But I'm not. In fact, I can't stop smiling.

I imagine my beautiful Melissa, her belly swelling with the baby we made. I can't even name all the things I'm feeling. I'm worried, and amazed, and more than a little bit scared. But more than anything, I'm overcome with an overwhelming desire to protect her. I want to wrap her in my arms and keep her safe. I want to watch over her while she nurtures our baby. I don't want her out of my sight.

It's late, and I'm in no state to get behind the wheel, so I text my driver. I know Melissa won't see me tonight, but I'm not going to stay a hundred fifty miles away from her. I'll go to Jetty Beach, get a hotel, and figure out what to do.

This is something I can't fix—but I don't want to. I have no idea how this happened to me. Tammi and Dennis are right: I'm in love with her. It feels good to admit it, even just to myself. I'll tell her, as soon as she lets me see her. I'll tell her I love her, and I want to be there for her, and our baby. I'll find a way to show her that I'm serious. That I can change. That I'm in this for the long haul, no matter what happens.

I throw a few things in a bag and text Dennis to tell him I'm leaving. I'll sneak out the back way, so I don't get caught up among the people downstairs. They can stay as long as they want. They can all fucking pass out and go home in the morning for all I care. None of them matter.

The only thing that matters is my woman, and the baby inside her.

26

MELISSA

I sit in a booth at the Old Town Café, picking at a blueberry muffin. Nicole's across from me, typing on her laptop, a half-finished cup of coffee on the table next to her. I take a sip of my own coffee. I guess I'm not supposed to drink caffeine while I'm pregnant, and I've cut back to one or two a day. But there's no fucking way I'm giving up coffee entirely. *Sorry, kid.*

Nicole agreed to meet me for lunch, although she warned me she had work to do. I don't mind. Mostly I don't want to be alone. I visited my dad this morning and told him about the baby. I cried so hard, I barely got the words out. He wrapped me in his strong arms, his flannel shirt itching my skin, and held me.

To my amazement, he wasn't angry or disappointed. He wanted to know what he could do—how he could help. He assured me I'll be all right, and even though the circumstances aren't ideal, he's thrilled to be expecting a grandbaby. That only made me cry harder.

I touch the skin beneath my eyes, wondering if I'm still all red and blotchy. Nicole hasn't mentioned it, but maybe she's just being polite. She just hugged me tight and offered to buy my lunch. I'm not very hungry, and she cast a weird glance my direction when all I ordered was coffee and a muffin. I guess she thinks I'm supposed to be eating my weight in food already. At this point, I still don't feel much of anything. Maybe I'm a little more tired than usual, but other than that, I can't even tell I'm pregnant.

I definitely did not take five more pregnancy tests to be sure. Nope.

"So," she says, closing her laptop. "How are you feeling?"

"Fine. I guess that's weird? But I feel pretty normal."

She shrugs. "I supposed it's different for everyone. I'm still trying to wrap my head around this. Although that's stupid of me to say. I can only imagine how it must be for you."

"Yeah, it's very surreal. I look at myself in the mirror and I can't see it, you know? I look the same, and I feel the same."

"You don't look the same, though."

"I don't?" I touch the skin under my eyes again. "I look like shit, don't I?"

"No. You look really good, actually. Your skin looks amazing. I think pregnancy suits you."

"Shut it, Jacobsen."

Nicole giggles. "I'm not a Jacobsen yet. Come to think of it, you'll have the baby by the wedding, won't you? Wow."

I blow out a breath. I've been thinking about those things. By *this* date, I'll be really pregnant. By *this* date, I'll have a three month old. "It's so weird. None of it feels real."

"So, you never told me what Jackson said when you told him," she says, lowering her voice. "You told him, right?"

"Yeah, I told him."

"And?"

I take another sip of my coffee. "I don't know. He was shocked. He dropped the phone and I thought he hung up on me. He said a bunch of stuff about wanting to be there and shit."

"He did? Melissa, that's great."

I draw my eyebrows together. "Is it? Why is that great?"

"Are you serious?"

"Yes. He's Jackson Bennett. He's a player, not a father."

"Why aren't you giving him any credit?"

"Credit for what? Knocking me up? He can have all the credit for that."

"Did he say he doesn't want anything to do with you?"

"No."

"Did he say he'd pay you a bunch of money if you'd go away?"

"No."

"Did he say he wanted to help?"

"Well, yeah, he kind of did."

"And what did you say?"

I stare at the table, not answering.

"Mel, what did you tell him?" she asks.

"I told him he didn't need to do anything, and I only called him so he'd know what was going on. And then I hung up."

"Really? And you don't think you're being the slightest bit unfair to the guy?"

"Why are you on his side all of a sudden?" I ask, prickling with anger.

"Do there have to be sides? I'm just telling you what I see. I'm sure he's as shocked as you are. Why don't you at least give him a chance to do the right thing?"

"What does that even mean? Do the right thing. Should I expect him to give up his lifestyle for this? If I do that, I know what will happen. He'll get bored. He'll suffocate under the responsibility. And he'll leave."

"Why are you so sure of that?"

"Why are you so sure he won't?"

"I'm not. Maybe you're right about him. You know him better than I do. But you aren't being honest with yourself about him either."

"What is that supposed to mean?"

"You fell for him, hard. And somehow I don't see you falling for a guy who would abandon you like that. Yeah, he's been a player or whatever, but he wasn't with you. You guys said a week, but neither of you wanted it to end there. And it was you who pushed him away, not the other way around. He's been trying to be in your life since you guys got back. That doesn't seem like a man who sees you as nothing but a meaningless fling."

Damn it. I hate it when she's right. "How am I supposed to deal with his life? I had to abandon my house and hole up in a hotel room with a fucking security guard. What the hell is that?"

"Yeah, that was nuts. I don't know, Mel. I don't know how you make that work, or even if you can. But you're having his baby, and nothing's going to change that now. You should give him a fair chance to be that baby's father."

I don't answer, picking at my muffin in silence. Nicole opens her laptop again and starts typing.

We sit quietly for a while. Maybe Nicole has a point. Jackson's reaction could have been a hell of a lot worse. How could he not be surprised? It isn't like I squealed with joy when I found out. Did I expect him to be happy? He immediately said he wanted to help—that he wasn't going to walk away.

The truth is, I'm afraid to let him in. He's a man with two

assistants, who has an entire floor of his building just for throwing parties, who's invited to posh banquets with celebrities, and has to think about photographers and private security. I'm just his mysterious sassy girl, a bit of fun he could brag about on social media.

Aren't I?

I'm not giving him enough credit, but I'm not sure I can face him either.

I glance up to find Nicole looking past me, her eyes wide.

"What's wrong?"

"Don't look, he's here," she says, the words tumbling out quickly.

My back clenches. Oh fuck. "Jackson?" I ask, whispering.

Her eyes are locked on something, or someone, behind me. She nods and mouths *He's coming.*

Jackson stands next to our table, close enough that I could touch him. My traitor body reacts immediately, the first whiff of his fresh cologne sending a tingle up my spine. He looks perfect, as usual, in an aqua button-down shirt with the sleeves cuffed, and gray slacks.

"Hi Nicole," he says. "Melissa, can I talk to you?"

He nods toward another booth. Nicole mouths an emphatic *Go* at me.

I follow him to the back of the restaurant and slide into the booth. He sits across from me. His gaze is so intense, and there's something in his face I've never seen before. I'm used to him staring at me, but not like this.

"What are you doing here?" I ask.

"How are you?"

I sigh at the urgency in his voice. "I'm fine. I mean, I'm *pregnant*, but other than that, I'm fine." I emphasize the word on purpose. I want to see if he reacts.

His lips turn upward in the slightest of smiles.

"Yeah, but how are you feeling?"

"I feel okay. I don't really feel different at all. Not yet."

"Okay, good," he says, his shoulders relaxing.

"When did you get into town?"

"A few days ago. It's been so hard not to see you, but I wasn't sure if you'd be ready to talk to me yet."

"And you picked today?"

"I was out and I saw your truck. Listen, I've been doing a bunch of research. I found a doctor in Seattle, she's one of the best in the country—"

"What?" I ask, cutting him off.

"A doctor, I—"

"Why are you looking for a doctor. For me?"

"Of course. You'll need a good doctor. I want you to have the best. The hospital down here is rated okay, but there's a birthing center in Seattle that I thought you might want to tour. It seems all peaceful and stuff, but if you want a regular hospital, there's one really close to my condo. You probably have insurance, but you don't need to use it. I'll cover everything. I already opened up a trust that will cover college, and I adjusted for projected inflation. That way if anything happens to me or my businesses, that will be taken care of. Your truck won't really work with a car seat, so I was thinking I'd buy you a—"

I put up a hand, cutting him off again. "Jackson, stop."

"What?"

"You don't have to buy me a car."

"Yes, I do."

"No, you don't."

"Melissa, I want to do the right thing."

I slump in my seat. "Thank you, Jackson. I don't want you to think I don't appreciate it. You're not buying me a car, but the rest is fine, I guess. I can find my own doctor, so don't worry about that. You can pay for whatever. It's fine."

"What do you want me to do? Tell me, and I'll do it."

"I don't want you to do anything. I want you to live your life and be happy. I don't want to be a burden on you, and there's no way that this isn't, so I guess I'm stuck with that."

"It's not a burden."

"Of course it is."

"I'm not running away from this," he says. "I'll step up."

Tears sting my eyes, and my stomach rolls over. "I'm already a mistake you'll have to live with for the rest of your life. I'm not going to make it worse."

I can't look at him anymore. His eyes are so intense. I don't want his money, but if it makes him feel better to buy things, I'll let him do it. I just can't sit here with him, fighting back tears, feeling like I'm being torn apart from the inside. I can't be the one to ruin his life.

"Melissa, you're not—"

I get up and run out the door.

27

JACKSON

That went monumentally worse than I feared.

I lean back against the booth and press my hands over my eyes. Fuck. How did I screw that up so badly? What did I do wrong? I'm here. I'm ready to take care of everything. What more does she want from me?

I look up to see Nicole standing next to the booth.

"Hey," she says. "Can I sit?"

"Sure." I lean forward and put my elbows on the table.

Nicole sits, putting her purse and a laptop case on the bench seat beside her. "This is really none of my business. But I can't sit there and do nothing."

"Shouldn't you be going after her or something? You guys can go somewhere and talk about what a shithead I am."

"No, she needs to be alone. I've known her long enough to know that."

"I don't know what just happened."

"She's scared. There isn't a lot that scares Mel, so she's kind of in uncharted territory. Maybe she's not handling it so well."

"I know she's scared," I say. "I am, too. I'm scared as fuck, but I'm here."

"Yeah, you are."

Does she seem impressed? Or surprised?

"I thought I had it all figured out. I found her a doctor, and I'll replace her truck so she can fit a car seat, and I funded a trust for college. This is what I can do, Nicole. I can take care of her."

She nods. "Sure, you can do all that. And it's good. I'm not gonna lie, I'm impressed. I know I don't know you very well, but when she first told me, I kind of thought ... I don't know, like you'd try to get out of this somehow."

"That's apparently what she thinks too."

"No, it isn't," she says. "But it *is* what she's afraid of."

"Why?"

"Well, you guys haven't known each other very long. It's been, what, a couple of months at the most? Now she's facing this huge change, and she's afraid it's going to be too much for you. She's steeling herself for you to walk out, so it doesn't hurt so much if you do."

"I'm not walking out. I don't want to. Fuck, I'd do anything for her. You know what, maybe I'll go buy a minivan. That will show her I'm serious."

"A minivan?" She raises her eyebrows.

"Yeah. A nice family car."

"What are you going to do, roll up in front of her house in your daddy-wagon?"

"Yes," I say, brightening. "Exactly."

"Oh my god, don't."

"Why?"

"Are you Richard Gere?"

"What?"

"Is she a prostitute?"

"What the fuck are you talking about?" I ask.

"No? Then stop trying to reenact *Pretty Woman*. A white limo and roses, or a white minivan, are not what she needs from you."

"Then what does she need? I thought I could show her I mean it."

"Would you be here if she wasn't pregnant?"

"Yes," I say, without hesitating. "Maybe it wouldn't have been today. But I wasn't going to let her go, even before I knew." I take a deep breath, like I'm about to jump into deep water. "I love her."

Holy fuck, I said it out loud.

Nicole's eyes widen. "Are you serious?"

"I've never been more serious."

She puts a hand to her mouth, smiling behind her fingers. "This is like, I don't even know. You love her?"

It's such a relief to be able to just say it. "I fucking love the shit out of her."

Nicole laughs. "Wow, okay. I like you way more than I did five minutes ago. Here's the thing. She doesn't want you to do the right thing, or swoop in and take care of her. Not right now, anyway. She's scared because she doesn't want to hold you back. She doesn't want to be an obligation. And she's convinced herself that even if you're here now, it's only because you feel like you have to be. Not because you want to be. Not because you want *her*. And it won't be long before you leave."

"But I do want her. I've never wanted anything like this before. My life is shit without her."

"Then you need to tell her. Whatever moment you're trying to create, it isn't about you. It's about *her*. You need to show her in a way that's meaningful to Melissa."

"How do I do that?

"Just, be you," she says with a shrug. "She loves you too, whether she wants to admit it or not. That's why she's so afraid to let you back in. She doesn't want you to solve her problems. She needs to know you love her, for *her*, and you want to be with her. She needs to know how you feel."

A calmness settles over me. I sit back in my seat, thinking about the details. I know exactly what to do. I'll have to go back to Seattle first, but it will be worth it.

"Thank you, Nicole," I say, getting up from my seat.

"Wait, where are you going?"

"I'll be back. Keep an eye on her while I'm gone, okay?"

I leave Nicole gaping at me, and go outside to call my driver.

28

MELISSA

I'm pretty sure Nicole is avoiding me.

Ever since Jackson showed up at the café, she's been acting weird. I have dinner at her place, with Ryan, Cody, and Hunter, and she barely speaks to me. I know it's because she talked to Jackson. I've seen no sign of him since. He probably told her he was out, that this whole thing was too much hassle, and she doesn't have the heart to tell me.

After that, she takes forever to answer my texts. When I suggest hanging out the next day, she has some excuse about doing wedding stuff. It might be legit—I'm probably being overly sensitive. But it seems odd. As soon as I told her I was pregnant, she went into full-on circle-the-wagons mode. Now she's too busy to hang out?

I curl up on my couch, a blanket over my legs, and try to pay attention to the book I'm reading. I've read the same page at least four times, and I still can't remember what happened. I give up, tossing the book to the side, and grab the remote. I flip on the TV and fire up Netflix. My go-to is usually *Firefly*, but I don't think I can watch it again. All I can think about is that first night in San Diego, when Jackson was so sweet. He made me tea. I glance at my steaming mug, the little string from the tea bag hanging off the side. Fuck it, I can drink tea and not think about him. I can still watch a show.

I doze off about halfway through the first episode, the familiar lines running through my mind. A knock at the door startles me. My curtains are closed, so I can't see who's outside. It's probably Nicole. I get up, pushing the blanket aside, hoping she brought takeout. I'm starving.

My appetite vanishes as soon as I open the door. It's Jackson.

"Hi." His eyes sparkle in the sun. "Will you come for a drive with me?"

I glance down at my clothes. I'm wearing a pair of black leggings and a long t-shirt, an even longer tank layered beneath it. I touch my hair—I'm pretty sure I brushed it earlier.

"Um, I guess so."

He smiles and steps aside. I grab my purse from the little table next to the door, slip on a pair of sandals, and follow him out to his car.

He has the Bugatti, no driver in sight. It's still the most comfortable car I've ever been in, but I can't enjoy it. I'm too anxious. Why is he here?

He pulls out onto my street and turns the corner, not saying a word. It's fucking weird. He's never this quiet. We drive south, down toward the edge of town. I keep expecting him to start talking, to fill the silence. He seems oddly relaxed. I'm the one who can't stop fidgeting, bouncing my leg up and down.

"Where are we going?"

He doesn't answer.

We pull down a beach approach and he moves the car off to the side.

"What are we doing here?"

He just smiles at me and gets out of the car.

He waits at the front of the car, his hands in his pockets, his face maddeningly serene. What the hell is going on with him? When I get out, he turns and walks down the beach. I follow. What else am I supposed to do?

The sun shines; a few puffy white clouds amble across the sky. The waves crash along the beach, white foam bubbling. Jackson stops where the deep dry sand turns hard-packed and wet. I step up beside him, my patience at his silence fading fast.

"Jackson, what are we doing out here?"

He looks at me, and my heart nearly bursts. There's no sign of the cocky show-off. No confident smirk of a man used to getting everything he wants. His eyes are intense, his expression utterly serious.

"We're out here because I want to talk to you alone."

There's no one else in sight. No cars. No one out for a stroll. Not even any footprints in the sand.

He pulls out his phone and holds it up. I open my mouth, the words *Don't you dare take my picture right now* on my lips. But before I can speak, he hurls it out into the water.

"Why did you do that?" I ask, aghast.

"No pictures, no tweets. No audience."

My heart beats faster and a tingle of nervousness runs through my belly. Or is that a pregnancy thing?

"Melissa."

The way he says my name. So forlorn. So passionate.

"Yes?"

"I've never met anyone like you. You're fierce and strong, but gentle and soft. You're fearless, not afraid to tell me what you want. I knew, sitting next to you in that bar, there was something different about you. That's why I wanted you. I used to be surrounded by all kinds of women, but none of them meant anything. I didn't think anyone ever would. Until I met you."

I swallow hard, hugging my arms around myself.

"You're right that we come from different worlds," he continues. "I don't know what it's like to grow up here, or have a father who gives a shit. You don't know how to deal with the media, and assholes who think they're entitled to a view of your private life. But, I just..." He pauses, looking away. "That stuff doesn't matter to me. No, that's not true. It *does* matter. But not enough to keep me away from you. When I asked you to go away with me, I thought I was going to sweep into your life and blow you away. But the truth is, the opposite happened. You blew me away. You changed me. Or maybe it wasn't a change—maybe you found something that was already there, waiting for the right person to bring it out."

He pauses again, but I can't speak.

"This has been a whirlwind, I know," he says. "And we're both in a place we didn't expect to be. But I'm not even kidding when I tell you this—I wouldn't have it any other way."

"You don't mean that."

"Yes, I do," he says, stepping closer. "We're going to have a baby together, Melissa. That's all kinds of crazy—but fuck, it's wonderful."

Tears burn my eyes. He can't be serious.

"You're afraid I'm going to get bored, or stifled by you. You know what was stifling me? Believing that all that bullshit I was doing made me happy. I've never been happier than when I'm with you. I don't want anything else. I love you, Melissa. I fucking love you so much I can barely breathe."

I put a hand over my mouth. I should say something, but I can't get a word out.

He reaches into his pocket and pulls out a small box. Despite myself, I gasp. Confusion swirls through me. The box is faded, the edges worn. This isn't a box from a luxury jewelry store. I can barely make out the logo on the top.

Jackson Bennett wouldn't propose without a fancy ring. That isn't his style. He'd find the biggest, gaudiest diamond imaginable. Wouldn't he?

"Open it."

My hands tremble as I take the lid off the box. Inside is a softer box, its velvety surface in better condition. Baffled, I slip it out of the cardboard and open the lid.

I almost drop it. Inside is a slim gold ring with a tiny diamond in a simple setting.

My mother's wedding ring.

Tears run down my face. How did he get this? How did he even know it existed?

I swallow and take a shaky breath. "Where did you get this?"

"It's a funny story, actually. After I last saw you, I left town and went back to Seattle, intending to buy you the biggest fucking ring I could find. That would show you, right? Except, when I got there, I looked around and none of them were you. It wouldn't have mattered how much money I dropped on one of those stupid things. I realized that isn't what you want from me. This is something my money can't buy. So, I spoke to your father."

"My dad?"

Jackson nods. "Yesterday. I went to him in person. I asked if he might still have your mother's ring, and if he'd be willing to let me propose to you with it."

"I can't believe you talked to my dad."

"You told me he was old-school. I wasn't going to ask you to marry me without his permission."

Oh my god, is this really happening?

"He gave you my mother's ring?"

"Yes," Jackson says, his voice so soft. "He probably won't admit it now, but he cried a little."

A sob shakes my shoulders. My dad cried? I saw my dad cry once in my entire life, long ago, when I was a little girl. The pain I saw in that moment took root in my soul and never truly left.

"Melissa, I'm standing before you, just a man. Not a suit or a bank account. Not a solution to your problems. Just a man who loves you with everything he is. I don't know how much that's worth. But you're worth everything to me."

He moves in close and lifts my hands. The box is still sitting in my palm.

No glitz. No flash. No waving money in my face.

"Until I met you, I didn't know I was capable of loving anyone," he says, his voice quiet. "But I love you. And if you let me, I'll love you forever. Melissa, will you marry me?"

This. This moment. This was what I wanted. What I didn't dare to dream, because it didn't seem possible. Jackson, the façade stripped away. No hiding behind his money or his charm. Just him, real and open.

And he wants me.

His brow creases with worry.

Yeah, I'll let him sweat it for a few more seconds.

I hold his eyes and lift my left hand.

With a gentle touch, Jackson takes the ring from the box and slides it onto my finger.

"Yes."

EPILOGUE - MELISSA

"Ooh, that's mine," I say, grabbing a piece of steak from Jackson's plate with my chop sticks.

We're stretched out across the bed in the penthouse in the nicest hotel in Jetty Beach. We usually stay at my place when we're in town, but the septic tank backed up and I literally can't go anywhere near it. The smell makes me instantly nauseated. Besides, staying at a hotel isn't so bad. I don't mind not having to clean up after myself, and the sheets are spectacular.

We haven't quite figured out the logistics of where we live. Do we live in Seattle? In Jetty Beach? I'm not sure anymore, but it doesn't seem to matter. We spend time in both places and I kind of like our back-and-forth life.

The school year started, but I'm taking a sabbatical from work. Between the controversy, and my pregnancy, I decided to take the year off. I'm not sure if I'll return to teaching. At this point, I'm content to focus on the baby. And, to be fair, money isn't an issue. I figure I'm going to be a mom and I can take some time to figure out what my future will look like. It won't be long, and everything is going to change.

I rub the swell of my belly through my white t-shirt. I'm visibly pregnant, although I still have almost four months to go. People usually assume I'm further along—apparently the baby has nowhere else to go but out. Nicole can't stop talking about how cute I am, and she gives Ryan a lot of longing looks. I think I'm making him very, very nervous.

My ring sparkles in the light. I still love looking at it. We got married in Vegas a month ago, although we haven't told anyone. We sneaked into a chapel with sunglasses and hoods over our heads to avoid anyone with a stray camera, and an Elvis impersonator did the honors.

It was completely perfect. I love having such a big secret that only Jackson and I share. Dennis is planning a real wedding for us late next year. I don't want mine to overshadow Nicole's, and I'd kind of like to have wedding pictures where I'm not hugely pregnant. Of course, there will be a baby in those pictures, but it isn't like the kid won't be able to do the math someday and figure it out.

"Hey, you wanted the chicken," Jackson says, frowning at me when I take another piece of steak from his plate. He plucks a bit of meat from mine.

"Oh, hell no. You do not take food from a pregnant woman."

He grins at me and puts the chicken back. The takeout boxes are set on a wooden tray, along with bottled iced teas. He moves everything down to the floor and scoots closer to me.

"Is lunch what you wanted?" He leans in and kisses his way down my collar bone, his hand lingering on my breast.

"Mm, you need to stop that. I'm starving."

The only thing stronger than my appetite for food is my appetite for sex. My hormones are on fire, and Jackson has no qualms about my changing body. If anything, he enjoys it in new ways. He particularly loves my boobs—but let's be honest, they look amazing. If my belly has to get huge, at least I get bigger boobs out of the deal.

He gently takes the plate from my hands and sets it aside, his mouth never far from mine. I'm hungry, but what the hell, the food will be here later.

I let him press me back onto the bed. He slides his hand beneath my skirt. I moan as he nudges my legs apart, his fingers working their magic.

"I guess you're not freaked out," I say.

He nuzzles against my neck, nibbling my skin.

We had our first ultrasound this morning. Seeing that tiny little figure moving around on the screen was one of the most intense moments of my life. I already feel such a bond to this little person; I can't explain it. I don't even know if it's a boy or a girl, but I already love this baby with a fierceness that kind of takes my breath away.

"Of course I'm not freaked out." He pushes his fingers in harder, rubbing up and down. I fumble for his pants, trying to free his cock.

Jackson is as attached as I am. He caresses my belly constantly. He leans down and talks to the baby, insisting he needs to make sure he or she knows his voice. I even caught him reading a parenting book when he thought I wasn't looking.

Whatever fears I had that Jackson would spook and leave me are gone. He positively dotes on me, even when I don't want him to. I had to convince him I don't need the fucking secret service when I go places by myself. But I have to admit, his protective side is sexy as hell.

He stops before I can get his pants down and props himself up next to me. "Were you worried I'd freak out?"

I take a deep breath, my whole body tingling. "I don't know, not really. But why did you stop?"

He smiles and trails a finger down my leg. I feel a little flutter as the baby shifts. It is the weirdest thing, to feel something moving in my belly and realize it's a *person*. This pregnancy is so out of the blue, and so very unplanned—I never contemplated what it would be like to have a baby growing inside me. It's strange and surprising and wonderful, and often very emotional, all at once. I've never laughed and cried so much—often at the same time.

"Do you regret not finding out the sex?" he asks.

We debated whether we wanted to know if it's a boy or a girl. I think we were both on the fence and at the last minute decided to wait until the baby's born.

"Do you regret it?"

Jackson gives me that gorgeous devil smile of his. "Maybe."

"Maybe? I thought we were in this together."

"Do you regret it?"

He definitely has something up his sleeve. "Maybe."

He gets up from the bed and pulls an envelope from his jacket.

"What is that?"

He sits down next to me and doesn't say anything, just puts the envelope on the bed between us.

"Jackson." I try to sound stern, but I'm smiling too much. I scoot so I'm sitting up—it isn't easy—and pull the sheets over my lap.

"I have not looked at this. You can see it's still sealed."

"But?"

"But I asked the doctor to write us a little note that we can either open, or not."

I groan. "That is so mean! I was all set to wait, and now

you have the answer sitting there in front of me? How am I supposed to resist that?"

"Let's not resist."

I lick my lips, staring at the envelope. Should we? "Fuck it. I'm in."

He tucks his finger underneath the flap and runs it along the edge, taking his damn time about it. My heart thumps with excitement, and the baby does a little roll. I put my hand on my belly. He makes a show of pulling out the folded piece of paper, a positively evil glint in his eyes.

"Damn it, let me see."

With maddening slowness, he unfolds the paper, smirking at me the whole time.

Suddenly his face falls, the smile disappearing. His eyes get wide and he swallows hard.

"What?" I ask, suddenly afraid. "What is it?"

He stares at the paper, blinking his eyes. He looks up, meeting my gaze, and passes the paper to me. Are there tears in his eyes? There can't be.

I take the note and smooth it out. In messy script, but plain as day, is a single word, and suddenly I know why Jackson looks like he's about to cry.

Girl.

AFTERWORD

Dear reader,

I'm just going to be honest. I love the shit out of this book.

Melissa was a natural choice for the next heroine in the Jetty Beach series and it was the title that came to me first. Must Be Crazy. What would be crazy? What would be something that would totally throw Melissa off her game?

Aha! Jackson Bennett. A rich playboy who presents her with an offer she can't refuse. A week with him. And as she tells herself, she's single, and she could use a little crazy in her life. Why not? What could possibly go wrong?

She might say a lot went wrong, but of course a lot more went right.

Melissa is a firecracker. I loved her combination of spunk and I-don't-give-a-fuck-ness. I got to indulge in my sailor mouth a little more than usual with her, and I won't lie, that was fun. Her commercial fisherman daddy, John Simon, was inspired by my in-laws, who have been fishermen for countless generations. John's comment about 'old fisherman and bold fisherman' is a direct quote from my wonderful father-in-law.

Jackson will always hold a special place in my heart. I feel like I took a risk writing him. Billionaire romances are such a THING, and they're tons of fun. But Jackson, despite being the sort of rich that begins with a B, is not typical for that role. He's not brooding and dark. He doesn't have a weird fetish. He doesn't need her to sign a contract.

He is confident, bold, and totally crazy for Melissa from the first time they meet. And that was what made him so utterly delightful to write. Here is this shark of a businessman (I know we don't get to see him work very much, because that wasn't what this story was about, but there's a reason he has so much money), who goes all soft and sweet for a woman. His appeal isn't in the cold, hard exterior. It's in the way he's completely taken with her. I loved writing a man who is flat out nuts for his woman, and has no idea he's actually in love.

These two were crazy fun to write (see what I did there?). Although I always intended to write the Jetty Beach books as stand-alones, I was tempted to draw this one out. I enjoyed both of these characters so much. I'm going to miss them!

Thanks for reading!

CK

ALSO BY CLAIRE KINGSLEY

For a full and up-to-date listing of Claire Kingsley books visit www.clairekingsleybooks.com/books/

For comprehensive reading order, visit www.clairekingsleybooks.com/reading-order/

The Haven Brothers

Small-town romantic suspense with CK's signature endearing characters and heartwarming happily ever afters. Can be read as stand-alones.

Obsession Falls (Josiah and Audrey)

The rest of the Haven brothers will be getting their own happily ever afters!

How the Grump Saved Christmas (Elias and Isabelle)

A stand-alone, small-town Christmas romance.

The Bailey Brothers

Steamy, small-town family series with a dash of suspense. Five unruly brothers. Epic pranks. A quirky, feuding town. Big HEAs. Best read in order.

Protecting You (Asher and Grace part 1)

Fighting for Us (Asher and Grace part 2)

Unraveling Him (Evan and Fiona)

Rushing In (Gavin and Skylar)

Chasing Her Fire (Logan and Cara)

Rewriting the Stars (Levi and Annika)

The Miles Family

Sexy, sweet, funny, and heartfelt family series with a dash of suspense. Messy family. Epic bromance. Super romantic. Best read in order.

Broken Miles (Roland and Zoe)

Forbidden Miles (Brynn and Chase)

Reckless Miles (Cooper and Amelia)

Hidden Miles (Leo and Hannah)

Gaining Miles: A Miles Family Novella (Ben and Shannon)

Dirty Martini Running Club

Sexy, fun, feel-good romantic comedies with huge… hearts. Can be read as stand-alones.

Everly Dalton's Dating Disasters (Prequel with Everly, Hazel, and Nora)

Faking Ms. Right (Everly and Shepherd)

Falling for My Enemy (Hazel and Corban)

Marrying Mr. Wrong (Sophie and Cox)

Flirting with Forever (Nora and Dex)

Bluewater Billionaires

Hot romantic comedies. Lady billionaire BFFs and the badass heroes who love them. Can be read as stand-alones.

The Mogul and the Muscle (Cameron and Jude)

The Price of Scandal, Wild Open Hearts, and Crazy for Loving You

More Bluewater Billionaire shared-world romantic comedies by Lucy Score, Kathryn Nolan, and Pippa Grant

Bootleg Springs

by Claire Kingsley and Lucy Score

Hot and hilarious small-town romcom series with a dash of mystery and suspense. Best read in order.

Whiskey Chaser (Scarlett and Devlin)

Sidecar Crush (Jameson and Leah Mae)

Moonshine Kiss (Bowie and Cassidy)

Bourbon Bliss (June and George)

Gin Fling (Jonah and Shelby)

Highball Rush (Gibson and I can't tell you)

Book Boyfriends

Hot romcoms that will make you laugh and make you swoon. Can be read as stand-alones.

Book Boyfriend (Alex and Mia)

Cocky Roommate (Weston and Kendra)

Hot Single Dad (Caleb and Linnea)

Finding Ivy (William and Ivy)

A unique contemporary romance with a hint of mystery. Stand-alone.

His Heart (Sebastian and Brooke)

A poignant and emotionally intense story about grief, loss, and the transcendent power of love. Stand-alone.

The Always Series

Smoking hot, dirty talking bad boys with some angsty intensity. Can be read as stand-alones.

Always Have (Braxton and Kylie)

Always Will (Selene and Ronan)

Always Ever After (Braxton and Kylie)

The Jetty Beach Series

Sexy small-town romance series with swoony heroes, romantic HEAs, and lots of big feels. Can be read as stand-alones.

Behind His Eyes (Ryan and Nicole)

One Crazy Week (Melissa and Jackson)

Messy Perfect Love (Cody and Clover)

Operation Get Her Back (Hunter and Emma)

Weekend Fling (Finn and Juliet)

Good Girl Next Door (Lucas and Becca)

The Path to You (Gabriel and Sadie)

ABOUT THE AUTHOR

Claire Kingsley is a #1 Amazon bestselling author of sexy, heartfelt contemporary romance and romantic comedies. She writes sassy, quirky heroines, swoony heroes who love their women hard, panty-melting sexytimes, romantic happily ever afters, and all the big feels.

She can't imagine life without coffee, her Kindle, and the sexy heroes who inhabit her imagination. She lives in the inland Pacific Northwest with her three kids.

www.clairekingsleybooks.com

Made in the USA
Columbia, SC
15 February 2024